Gonna Take
a Homicidal
Journey

Gonna Take
a Homicidal Journey

Sandra Scoppettone

LITTLE, BROWN AND COMPANY

Boston   New York   Toronto   London

First Edition

Library of Congress Cataloging-in-Publication Data

Scoppettone, Sandra.
    Gonna take a homicidal journey / Sandra Scoppettone. — 1st ed.
        p.   cm.
    ISBN 0-316-77665-3
    I. Title.
    PS3569.C586G66   1998
    813'.54 — dc21   97-44247

10 9 8 7 6 5 4 3 2 1

MV-NY

Published simultaneously in Canada by
Little, Brown & Company (Canada) Limited

Printed in the United States of America

This one is for Ray Roberts and Joe Blades,
two men who weren't afraid. I thank you.

Only one thing, however, is vividly present:
the constant tearing of the veil of appearances;
the constant destruction of everything in construction.
Nothing holds together, everything falls apart.

Eugène Ionesco

Gonna Take a Homicidal Journey

One

"If you hate it so much here, go back to town to your little girlfriend," Kip says.

Oh, boy. Here we go. She doesn't do it often but every now and then Kip throws Alex at me like a berserk bowling ball. Yes, I had an affair and Kip found out ("found out" . . . a euphemism for caught us) and it was dicey for a while but then we went to Sabena, a couples counselor, and we worked it out. I thought. Still, she hasn't completely forgiven me, that's clear.

"I have no little girlfriend, Kip. Please don't start that."

"You had one."

"*Had* is the operative word here."

Alex Thomas, whom I'd met once briefly, on a case, E-mailed me, and one letter led to another. And then we re-met in person. Kip was away and we hadn't been getting along. I don't know, maybe it was a midlife crisis, one of those Gail Sheehey passages, or maybe it *was* in reaction to Kip. At any rate, Alex and I had a short-lived affair.

I had been trying to end things with Alex and she wanted to be friends. Then Kip walked in on us, kissing. It's as vivid now as the day it happened.

"When we can be in a room together without wanting to kiss, then we can be friends," I said to Alex.

"Do you want to kiss me now?"

"Of course I do."

"So do I," she said and leaned toward me.

I couldn't resist that beautiful mouth and my lips met hers. All of my sexual feelings were aroused and I put my arms around her, drew her close to me, felt her breasts against mine. I knew where this was going to lead but I couldn't stop. Well, I'd warned her. I pulled away, ready to ask her to come upstairs to bed with me. But she had an odd look on her face.

"Turn around," she whispered.

"What?"

"Turn around."

I did.

Kip stood just inside the living room door, suitcase at her feet.

"Well, girls," she said tartly, "how long has this been going on?"

Oh, boy, I thought.

Alex got to her feet, face flushed. She didn't know what to say and neither did I.

"Going to introduce me?" Kip asked.

I had no idea what the protocol was for this situation, so that's what I did. They didn't shake hands.

"I think I'd better go," Alex said.

Kip said, "That seems like a sensible idea."

Alex, who didn't even glance my way, moved past Kip and out the door into the hall. Kip and I stared at each other until we heard the outside door close.

"I hope," Kip said, "you're not going to say, it's not what it looks like."

I shook my head. "It's exactly what it looks like."

"Lovely." Her brown eyes appeared more hurt than angry, and I desperately wanted to take her in my arms, erase the pain, go back in time, anything to make the truth go away.

Kip looked down at her suitcase. "Should I pick this up and leave?"

"Of course not." I walked toward her. She took a step back,

so I stopped. "If anyone should go, it's me," I said, hoping that wouldn't have to happen. "This is your house."

"Funny," she said, "I always thought of it as ours."

"Funny, I never felt that."

"Really?" She seemed genuinely surprised.

"Yes, really."

"I'm sorry . . . no, we're not going to switch this around. Maybe we'll talk about that later."

She walked past me and sat on the couch where Alex had been sitting, obviously waiting for me to speak.

I did. "It hasn't been going on long and it probably was in reaction to you."

She laughed. "So I'm going to be blamed for it, huh?"

"No, I don't mean it that way."

"Then how is it in reaction to me?"

"Kip, you've been absent for a long time. I don't mean now, while you've been physically away. I mean since your brother died. And I'm not saying what I did was right, it just happened."

"Ah, the adulterer's favorite words, 'It just happened.' "

I could see this was going to be a nightmare. And what did I expect?

"Are you in love with her?" Kip asked me.

"No. Of course not."

"What, then?"

I shrugged.

"Outstanding defense," she said.

"Look, Kip, I can't defend myself. It happened and now it's over."

"But it wouldn't be over if I hadn't come home early, hadn't walked in on you?"

"I know this sounds stupid, after what you saw, but I was trying to end it."

"You're right. It sounds stupid."

"I love you, Kip."

"Forgive me if I find that hard to believe."

"I'm sure you do. We need help. We needed help before this."

"Looks like you got help."

"That's not what I mean. We need professional help."

"Was she good in bed?"

Oh, boy. "Do you think this is going to be productive?"

"Spare me the jargon, Lauren."

"Everything I say sounds like a cliché. But . . ."

"Maybe because what you did is a cliché. God, Lauren, you're like some stupid middle-aged man going after a young, beautiful babe."

"She's not that young," I said inanely.

Kip shook her head as though I were an idiot. "So what do you want to do?"

"I want to work things out."

She sat quietly for what seemed like a lifetime. "It ain't gonna be easy."

"I know. But I want to try. Do you?"

"Yes."

We both started to cry.

I never saw Alex again although it was hard. She kept pushing the friendship angle but I couldn't do it. Maybe someday. More than six months have passed now and I still think of her, not with longing for Alex, per se, but with nostalgic feelings for the insanity that comes with having an affair, or any new love/lust. I have to admit I wonder if it will ever happen to me again. Or is this it, this life with Kip? Will we grow old and fat together (Kip won't), go stale, succumb to lesbian bed death? Will we end up in front of a television set eating on plastic TV tables?

Kip strikes through my dismal thoughts, says, "You're acting like you think taking time off was a mistake."

It had seemed like a good idea when the situation presented itself. And our couples counselor thought it would help us to get away, even though this isn't exactly a vacation.

Our friends Jenny and Jill bought a house in Seaview, on the North Fork of Long Island, and finally closed on it in mid-December. It was uninhabitable as it was and we agreed to help them start the renovations. So we all rented a big house in Hallockville (the town west of Seaview), on Long Island Sound, and prepared for demolition plus a little relaxation.

I say, "I think it's a mistake if you're going to start the Alex assault again."

Kip looks chagrined. "Sometimes I can't help it. I get this overwhelming feeling that you'd rather be with her."

"Well, I wouldn't. I'm simply not sure I want to be here." For one thing, I miss my computer. Part of the deal was that I leave it behind.

"C'mon, it'll be fun." She reaches out and touches my cheek.

I smile at her and my lover's heart does a swan dive when I see the old glint in her eyes. Moments like this make me know we were meant to be together and that we won't end up like chaste cellmates.

There were friends who thought she was crazy not to kick me out. But that would've been the easy road. The hard thing is to stick together and work it through. Hand in hand we leave our room and meet the Js in the kitchen.

I'm dressed in long underwear, sweatpants, three layers on top, and yellow work shoes. The other three are wearing approximately the same thing but somehow it looks better on them. Especially on Kip. Of course, she looks good in anything. Height makes all the difference. She's 5'6" to my 5'1". Jenny's my height and Jill is about 5'4". So why do they look better than I do? Perhaps it's attitude. I feel lumpen, the way I used to as a child stuffed in a snowsuit.

Kip says, "Are you sure they'll be all right while we're gone?"

The Js have Theo, a Welsh terrier, and we have Nick and Nora, two white Persian cats. It's a big house. This is day two and our pets are in separate rooms. They met once in the city, and there was a slight tussle over some food, but we won't make that mistake this time.

Tonight, when we come back from our first day of work on the Js' house, we will allow them to meet again. Kip can hardly wait. There's nothing that frightens her more than animal fights. I suspect it's because they're totally beyond her control, but I don't share my analysis with the others, as it might not be appropriate. Or safe.

"They have their own rooms," I say.

"You think Theo's going to get out, don't you, Kip?" asks Jenny. "And then you think she's going to open the door to Nick and Nora's room, go in, and eat them."

"Don't be silly," Kip says.

We all know this is exactly what she's thinking.

"*Eat* them?" she says, after a moment's pause. "Theo would eat them?"

"Kip, relax," Jill says. "She's gone off Persian cutlets."

Three of us laugh. Kip pretends to.

"Are we ready?" There's a look of panic on Jenny's cute face, as though she's about to encounter an executioner.

Jill shoves her red hair under a blue headband that covers her ears. "Please, Jen, don't start."

"What? What did I say?"

"It's the look," I put in.

"What look?"

"Buyer's remorse," we chorus.

"Let's face it, it's a dump," she says.

We each take our turn trying to convince her otherwise.

"It's a dump now, but when you get finished it'll be a show place."

"Think of the spot, the view, right on the water."

"By June you'll be thrilled with it."

"I don't know," Jenny says. "I think we made a stupid mistake."

We groan. We've heard all this a million times.

"Let's go," Kip says.

When we step outside, the wind coming off the Sound practically knocks us backward. I've never felt anything quite like it. We run across the deck and down the stairs to our cars. We've brought both, not wanting to be dependent on each other. Ours is a new red Jeep Cherokee Sport because the Range Rover was totaled months ago by an insane criminal. Theirs is a black Honda station wagon.

By the time I get in the Jeep my face feels like a block of ice. "Put the heater on," I say.

"Lauren, I haven't even started the car."

"Well, do it."

"You're impossible. It's not that cold. You don't know what cold is."

Oh no. I feel a narrative about her childhood in Michigan coming on. "You're right, I don't and I don't want to."

"This is nothing," she says, turning the key.

I check my impulse to reply. "Heater."

"How many times do I have to tell you it'll be cold if I turn it on now?"

"Three hundred and twenty-eight thousand."

"What?" she asks, bewildered.

"You asked me how many times did you have to tell me —"

"Don't," she warns. "Are you sure the cats will be all right?"

"Kip, I'm freezing and you're talking about the cats."

"What if Theo *does* get out?"

"And what? Turns the knob and opens the door to the cats' room?"

"It could happen."

"No, it couldn't. Heater, please."

"All in good time," says the sadist.

I stare at her as she backs out of the driveway. This is meant as a convincer but doesn't work. I give up, resigned to being cold for the next thousand years. I look past her at the Sound. The color is a deep green and the waves, beginning halfway to Connecticut, are ferocious. I hadn't expected waves on the Sound but there they are. I'm glad the house we've rented is not on the beach side of the street.

At last the brute turns on the heater. The air whooshes out of the vents, cold and unforgiving. So she's right, so what? I say nothing and pretend I don't notice.

We turn down Kimberly Road, cross Sound Avenue, and continue on until we come to the North Road. Here we take a left and head toward Seaview.

We don't go far before making a right at a small shopping center with a video store, a real estate agency, some food shop called a smokehouse, a Chinese take-out place, and the Big Bagel Deli. We need supplies. It's been at least an hour since breakfast.

The Js park next to us and we head for the deli. Yesterday we checked out the place, so we know the drill. It's one big room with white tables and white plastic chairs, a counter, and a coffee bar where you pour your own. There are customers scattered at the tables, reading papers and trading quips. Everyone seems to know everyone else.

The Js drink tea but Kip and I get large coffees then join the line to order. I already know that I'm going to have a cinnamon-raisin bagel with cream cheese.

"Now don't get a bagel slathered with cream cheese," Kip says to me.

I hate her. "I have to have something on it. You can't eat a bagel plain."

"Why not?"

"You're sick," I say.

"And you have a cholesterol problem."

"I'm not getting the chocolate bagel," I say defensively.

"What chocolate bagel?"

"The one I'd have if they made one."

"I'm not your mother," she says.

"Exactly. So don't tell me what to eat."

"I was telling you what *not* to eat." She smiles in that crooked way.

"Help you?" a woman says behind the counter.

"A seven-grain bagel, nothing on it," Kip says.

Eeeeuuu. Seven-grain . . . how does she even know they have something called that? Why must she be so healthy?

"Toasted?" the woman asks.

"No, slice it, please."

As I'm rethinking my choice, the door opens and slaps against the wall with a bang. We all look in that direction.

A man in his forties, wearing a red-billed cap, a black-and-red-checked woolen jacket, and jeans, stands there, his face stricken. The room is silent.

A woman behind the counter says, "What is it, Luke?"

"It's Bill Moffat."

"What about him?"

"They found him hanging in Ridley's Woods."

A collective gasp rises and all I can think is, *Let me out of here,* as visions of Jessica Fletcher dance in my mind.

Two

While we wait for our food, the talk of Bill Moffat continues. The Js look at me and roll their eyes heavenward. I shake my head, meaning: No way will I get involved in this.

Questions are hurled at Luke, the messenger, and he tries to answer, though he looks like he might faint.

He says, "Troy was taking a walk with his son, found him hanging from a tree."

"How long he been there?"

"No way to tell in this weather. Ed says he was like a human icicle."

Ed, I presume, is the medical examiner who can't tell yet how long Moffat has been dead.

"Suicide, I guess."

There's an angry chorus of "No."

Then: "Too much to live for."

"Wouldn't do that to Toby and the kid."

" 'Specially after Freddy."

"Right."

"Hey, I don't know. I'm telling you what I heard, is all," Luke offers.

"What's Chief Wagner say?"

"Don't know. Didn't see him."

The voices gradually calm down to a mumble, so the noise resembles what cicadas must sound like on a summer night in those *New Yorker* stories.

All of the counter people, three women and two men, are

bunched together whispering, and I see that not one has anything in a latex-gloved hand that looks like an order — our order.

Kip says, "Excuse me," to the woman who'd been waiting on us.

"Yes, dear?"

"Would it be possible to get our order now?"

"You're not from here," she says in an accusatory way.

"You mean, year-round?"

The woman nods solemnly and Kip follows suit, equally solemn.

"You didn't know Bill then?"

"No, I'm sorry."

The woman snaps her head like an exclamation point and asks again for our order. We comply (I get my bagel bare) and stand stupid and helpless while everyone around us discusses the death of a man named Bill Moffat. I try desperately not to, but I automatically file away bits and pieces of information.

When we finally get our breakfast Kip grabs me by my arm and leads me outside as if I were blind.

"Stop that," I say.

She lets go and we get in the Jeep.

As she turns the key she says, "We're on vacation, Lauren."

"Is this news?"

"Please don't get involved in this."

"Are you crazy?"

"No, but sometimes *you* are when it comes to crime."

"I have to be hired, Kip, and nobody here is going to hire me."

"Good."

We pull out of the parking lot, follow the Js onto the North Road, and head toward Seaview.

"I wonder if it was a suicide or murder?"

"You see? I knew it. You're going to get entangled."

Big mistake to have said this out loud.

"Can't a person speculate?"

"Of course, sorry. Let's forget about it. Look how beautiful it is."

We're passing the Sound again. "Mmmm."

"Oh, great nature lover," she says.

I have to admit, as I look past her at the public beach, there is a kind of bleak beauty. After that comes a stretch of motels, a restaurant called the Sound Vista, some small houses close to the highway, and then major houses — set far back from the road — which we can see because it's winter. Some houses sit high on bluffs and I can imagine how dazzling the view must be, how wonderful in summer, how cold right now. There's no way to determine which of these showplaces is inhabited except for an occasional car at the end of a long driveway.

"Wouldn't you love to live there?" Kip asks as we pass a mansion resembling Tara.

"Too small," I say.

"True. Where would we put Nick and Nora?"

"Exactly." I worry that she's getting the moving bug; worse, the buying bug. No matter where we go she always wants to move there.

"Maybe we should meet with some real estate agents while we're here," she says.

Oh, boy. "What for?"

"To see some houses."

Timorously, I ask, "For what reason?"

She glances over at me. "To look at, Lauren."

"To see if we want to buy something and move here and give up our entire way of life, right?"

"You don't have to view it that way."

"Kip, with you there's no other way to view it."

"Maybe we could rent a house for the summer."

"The *whole* summer?"

"People do go away on weekends in the summer, you know."

"What people?"

"Normal people."

"Whew, that leaves us out."

Before she can reply, the Js signal that they're going to make a right turn. When we follow I can't help noticing the street is Ridley's Lane. And that it's a wooded area. Ridley's Woods.

Kip notices too. "Don't even think about it."

It's hard not to because there are several police cars parked at the edge of the road and as I look to my right I see the familiar yellow crime-scene tape stretched between two trees across a dirt road. Suddenly I feel at home.

Ridley's Lane dead-ends at Route 25. Across the street is a 7-Eleven. We take a left, go a ways, hang a right, cross the railroad tracks, drive past some houses, and then: Ta-da! The Js' house.

We pull in the driveway behind them and all get out.

"Ohmigod," Jenny says, despondent.

"Jenny, don't," says Jill.

"What've we done?"

The house *is* small. And it isn't exactly pretty. There had been an outbuilding on the property, but at the Js' request, and part of the deal, the previous owner pulled it down and removed the concrete slab it sat on, so now they have an unobstructed view of the bay from their rear staircase! Just kidding. They plan to put in windows across the back of the house.

As we stand in the driveway we see the bay and a ferry going to Shelter Island.

"That's so beautiful," Kip says.

I agree.

"Hello there." A woman's voice from behind us.

We turn.

She has short white hair, a pleasant face, and is wearing a pink parka and orange sweats. "Are you the new owners?"

Jill says she is and shakes the woman's hand.

"I'm Bernadette, but everyone calls me Bernie. I live across the street." She points to a house covered in blue siding. "I wanted to thank you for giving me a view."

She's referring to the demolition of the outbuilding.

"I can't believe I can see the water. We've been here since

1957 and for the last ten years, because of that damn struc-ture, we had no water view. I bought this house on my lunch hour. It's true. I came home that night and said to my hus-band, 'I bought a house today.' " She has a laugh like apple butter. "Well, listen, I don't want to keep you. Welcome to the neighborhood. And by the way, my son does lawn work, you need someone. He does Liz and Kate's on Sixth Street, you want a recommendation. Thanks again. I'll see you soon." She crosses the street to her house.

We all look at each other.

"Liz and Kate?" Kip says, raising her eyebrows.

"Code," I say.

"Would you care to decipher it, sweets?"

"Liz and Kate. Not Bruce and Marilyn, for instance, or John and Jane. Two women. It's a way of telling you they know you're lesbians and they don't care."

"She's right," Jenny says.

"What would we do without a detective in our midst?"

Jenny says, "The porch goes first."

She's glaring at a small glassed-in front room with a glass door under rotting eaves.

"And then the inside walls," she adds. "And then we'll be dead."

"You're so cheerful," Kip says.

"Come on," Jill says in her usual sunny way. "Let's take a look."

"I've seen it," moans Jenny.

"Will you stop. This is our home," Jill states.

"Why do you think I'm crying?"

I can't help laughing. It's amazing how different they are from us but more amazing how similar we are. Jenny and I are alike in that we always see the worst, and Kip and Jill usually have an upbeat take on things. It gives us balance as couples and I guess in some ways this is what makes our relationships work.

We walk around to the back where a few stairs lead up to a postage-stamp porch. Jill unlocks the door and we file in.

"Ohmigod."

"Jenny, you act as if you've never seen this house before."

"I've never seen it since we paid for it," she says.

We're in the kitchen, which is small and has black-and-white linoleum squares covering most of the floor.

"It smells," Jenny says.

"I don't smell anything."

"Me either."

"There's definitely an odor," she continues.

Ignoring her, Jill says, "When we have the big window all across in back, it'll be terrific."

"It will be," I assure her, because it will.

We enter the biggest room of the house.

"Ohmigod. Jill, it's so dark."

The walls are pine-paneled and stained a dark mahogany. Three small bedrooms, equally dark, open off this space. The bathroom is not bad. Functional and easy to paint.

Jenny says, "We'll knock down all these inner walls and make it one big room."

Although I'm in the mood for demolition I can't help putting in my two cents. "Are you sure you want to do that before you live in it?"

"I couldn't live here this way."

"Hold on," I say. "If we paint everything white, and you have the kitchen done, put some furniture in here, you can live in it this summer and get a better idea of what you want."

Jill says, "It'll cost us a lot less right now if we do that."

"But more later," Jenny counters.

"That might be true but it still might be smart," says Kip.

"When we moved in to Perry Street we waited a year before we did anything, remember?" I say.

"So?"

"A lot of the ideas we had at first changed. If we'd done it right away we would've made mistakes."

"Yeah," Jenny says, ruminating. "I did that with our apartment and I've always been sorry. Jill, maybe they're right."

We look from one to the other, waiting.

"Demo or paint?" I ask.

"Paint," the Js duo.

"Hold everything, because we have to clean before we paint," Jill says.

Kip agrees. "C'mon. We need to buy soap, mops, paper towels, all that stuff."

Jenny and I groan. Sometimes I hate Jill and Kip. They're always right about things like this and they spoil all the fun.

Let's face it. We've gone from making dirt to cleaning dirt in a Seaview minute.

Three

━━━━━━━━━━━━━━━

We're exhausted by the time we get back to our house, having spent the day scrubbing walls and floors, scouring sinks, mining crust-covered windowsills, baseboards, and woodwork, then shopping for dinner.

Kip has rushed inside ahead of us, presumably to see if Theo has eaten Nick and Nora. When I finally get in the house she's smiling and none of the animals is present; obviously they're still in their respective quarters.

As we unpack the groceries we volunteer for (and, in some cases, assign) duties. Basically, I don't like to do anything. I especially hate cooking. Jenny loves it so she's going to make pasta with vegetables, Jill being a vegetarian. Jill will make the salad, Kip the dressing, and I will clean up. Somehow this doesn't seem equitable but who's keeping track?

"Jill, we should walk Theo."

"You mean, *I* should walk Theo."

"I'm cooking."

"I'm cooking, too."

"You're making the salad, Jill. Big deal."

"Fine," she says and goes off to Theo's suite.

Kip says, "I think I'll look in on the Ns."

She wants me to come with her to see if they're all right and I agree because all I want to do is sit down, and I can't until I change out of these filthy clothes.

The Ns have obviously heard us. They're both sitting in

front of the door when we open it. Nick gives his pitiful cry and Nora falls over onto her side.

"Oh, look at them," Kip says.

"I am looking at them."

She ignores me and gets down on the floor with them, speaking some cat language. I step over all three and head for the shower.

As we sit around the table, all of us cleaned up, the cats still in their lair, there is suddenly a terrible squawking sound. It takes a moment before we realize it's an alarm and that the house is filling with smoke.

The smoke's coming from the fireplace where Kip lit a fire earlier.

The alarm is not so easily located.

We jump up, shouting.

Theo barks.

"You have to open the flue."

"I did."

"So what's happening? Why is that smoke billowing in here?"

"Where's the goddamn alarm?"

Theo is barking.

"What should I do with the fire?"

"Throw water on it."

"There's the alarm. It's on the ceiling of the upstairs landing."

I run up the stairs. But this is stupid because there's no way I can reach the alarm. Nor could anyone else without standing on something. I rush down.

Theo is barking.

"A ladder. We need a ladder."

Kip is the tallest so she grabs a stool and awkwardly makes her way upstairs with it. We watch from below as she places the stool beneath the screeching alarm.

"She needs help," Jill says, and goes up.

Theo is barking.

Jill helps Kip get up on the stool and then holds on to her

as Kip opens the smoke detector, tries to shut it off, and finally, in desperation, yanks out the battery, which does the trick.

We give a collective sigh of relief. As Kip and Jill come down there's a knock at the door. We scream. This incident has worked our nerves.

"Who could it be?" Jenny asks suspiciously.

"The fire department?" I say.

When the knock repeats we manage not to scream but Jenny and I are rooted to our spots.

Theo is barking.

"Open the door," Kip says as she hits the last step, Jill behind her.

"Just open it?"

"Oh, really." Kip strides across the room. "We're not in New York, you know."

"You should ask anyway," I advise, but it's too late.

Kip pulls open the door, and a gust of cold air roars in. I can't see who it is from where I'm standing as she says: "Oh, hi, come on in."

It has to be someone she knows, but she doesn't know anyone here.

Yeah, she does. And so do we all. It's Mr. Volinewski, the real estate agent who found us this house.

"Sorry to bother you," he says as he comes in, a woman behind him.

Volinewski is in his fifties, a good-looking guy who sports a thin mustache and has blue eyes, the color of daylight, behind thin-rimmed glasses. He's over six feet, wears a tan parka, dark green cords, and chunky brown shoes.

Theo is jumping.

Volinewski leans over and pets her. "Hi there, pup. Is something burning in here?" he asks, sniffing.

"No, no," Kip says. "We built a fire and I don't know what happened but the smoke came out and —"

"You have to open the flue," he says.

Jenny says, "We did."

I know she's thinking, *Mr. Man doesn't think we know how*

to build a fire in a fireplace. I give her arm a squeeze and shake my head. She gets my meaning.

Theo is barking and jumping.

"Theo, stop," Jenny commands.

Theo doesn't.

"When it's windy outside sometimes it'll blow the damper closed at the top of the chimney."

"You mean," Jill asks, "we can't have a fire when it's windy?"

He shrugs.

"Oh, great," Kip says.

Jill says, "Theo, stop."

Theo does.

"I don't understand how you do that," Jenny says.

"I never rented this house in winter before. I didn't know. What can I say?"

How about sorry, I think.

Volinewski glances over at the table where our pasta is slowly growing cold. "Oh, we've interrupted your dinner. Maybe we should come back."

I can tell that this is a totally insincere offer.

"What can we do for you?" I ask, wondering why he's brought this silent woman with him and when he's going to introduce us.

"Well," he says, "when Jean called me I thought of you right away."

Ohbudofcourse, I think snidely. "Jean?" I say, trying to sound pleasant. Before he can answer, Kip asks them if they'd like to sit down and they leap at the offer, peel off their outer garments, and hang them on the coat tree. She leads them to the seating area of the living room.

There are two sofas and we squeeze in, Jill sitting next to Volinewski and the unknown woman. Because I'm a P.I. I suspect she's Jean.

"This is Jean Ashton," he says, gesturing toward the woman next to him. Remarkably, he introduces us all by our full names. I'm astonished that he remembers.

Jean is an attractive woman in her late forties, brown hair to her shoulders, eyes that match, an uneventful nose. She wears a charcoal crewneck sweater over a plaid flannel shirt and a red turtleneck. Her woolen slacks are black. I wonder if when she gets up she'll be covered with Persian fur. But then I remember the poor beasts haven't been out here yet.

"Mr. Volinewski —"

"Stash," he corrects. "It's my nickname. For Stanley."

"Stash," I say uneasily, "what exactly is it that we can do for you and Jean?"

"It's not for me," he says. "It's for Jean. And it's you specifically."

The Js and Kip stare at me and the music from *Jaws* plays in my head.

"I remembered that you're a . . . what, a private detective, right?"

Oh no. "Yes, I am."

"She's on vacation," Kip interjects.

I pinch her arm and she stifles a cry.

"What's the problem?" I ask.

Volinewski glances at Jean but she's clearly not about to say anything so he does it for her. "Well, Jean's got this cousin. Let's see. A kind of problem has arisen . . ."

"Oh, Stash," Jean says, impatiently. "They're saying my cousin killed himself and I know that can't be."

"Who's they?" I ask.

"The damn police. They don't know their ass from their elbow. Billy would never kill himself."

Billy. "Are you talking about the man in Ridley's Woods?"

Jean's eyes brighten as though no one has ever understood her before. "Yes. Billy Moffat. You heard, huh?"

"We were in a deli when somebody named Luke came in and told everybody."

Jean nods as if she can envision the scene. "What's Luke know? Nothing. Never did, never will."

"Is he a policeman?" I ask.

"Hell, no. He's the Seaview mayor. But he'll go along with whatever they say, not that it matters what Luke says or doesn't. Who matters is Chief Wagner. And Ed Conroy, the M.E. Conroy has no way of knowing so soon. Didn't any of them ever hear of lynching?"

The word ricochets around the room. *Lynching.* It's not something one expects to hear in this part of the country or century. "What do you mean?"

"What I mean is what I say. Billy was hung, he didn't hang himself."

"Who hung him?"

She looks at Volinewski, then slowly scans all our faces before her gaze comes to rest on me. "If I knew then I'd tell the police."

"You don't suspect anyone?"

"I didn't say that."

Jean wiggles around in her seat, looks at me. "You want the job?"

"*No,*" Kip blurts.

The room goes silent as everyone stares at her.

"Lauren, you promised."

"I did?"

"Yes. When we were driving from the deli to Seaview."

"It wasn't exactly a promise. Look, can we discuss this later, please?"

Volinewski says, "We should go. You have your dinner and all."

"Yes," says Jean. "I'll leave you my phone number and maybe you can call me later."

"I guess that would be better."

There is a lot of moving around, mumbling, and the putting on of coats. Jean writes her number down, we shake hands, and they leave. Kip is still sitting on the couch. Jenny and Jill are back at the table, where I join them.

"Aren't you going to eat, Kip?"

"It's cold, isn't it?"

"We can reheat it in the microwave."

"I've lost my appetite," she says.

"Can you at least sit here so we can talk this over?"

Her sigh is like the sound of the *Titanic* going under. Slowly she gets up and, as only Kip can, martyr-walks to the table, where she slumps into her chair beside me. I want to applaud but resist. I know there's the perfect approach to this but I don't know what it is. I don't want to fight, especially not in front of the Js (although we have and it hasn't done any irreparable damage), and I don't want Kip to be unhappy. But there's such a disparity between how much money each of us makes that I feel I should take a job whenever I can.

"Here's how I see it."

"I *know* how you see it, Lauren."

I ignore this. "We're no longer doing demolition on the house. It's only a matter of painting and —"

"What does the house have to do with it?" Kip asks.

"I'm not needed in the same way."

"Oh, I see. You mean if we were doing demo we'd need your brute strength?"

"Very funny. No, what I mean is . . . three of you painting is plenty and I have a chance to make some money."

"You know what you are, Lauren?" Kip asks.

If ever I heard a setup this is one. I don't answer.

It doesn't stop her. "You're an obsessed person."

Oh, that. "I thought you'd like it if I was obsessed with money."

"You're not obsessed with money, and no, I wouldn't like it if you were. You're obsessed with your job."

"Guilty as charged," I agree.

"It's true we're here to help the Js but this is also a vacation," Kip adds.

"Taking the job won't change anything."

"Oh, puh-leeze," they chorus.

"I'll try not to let it, okay?"

"You're going to do what you want anyway," Kip says.

Right. "I don't even know if I'll take this job."

"You'll take it. At least try to be around at night, will you?"

"I promise," I say, and blow her a kiss. "Want me to heat up your food?"

She gets a funny look. "Yes. In fact, I think you should be my slave while we're here."

"That's fair," Jenny says, grinning.

"Sounds right," Jill agrees.

I'd acquiesce to anything right now but have no intention of fulfilling that particular demand. So I lie a little; I never said I didn't. "Okay," I say. "I'll start right after I call Jean Ashton."

Four

Early in the morning, Kip goes to work on the Js' house in their car and leaves me the Jeep. I am to meet Jean Ashton at her home as soon as I can get there. Before I leave I find myself wandering around the empty house thinking I've forgotten to do something but not knowing what. The animals are safely tucked away, so it's not that.

Ah!

E-mail. I would normally be collecting it before going out. When I told Kip how it would pile up if I didn't bring the notebook, she pointed out that if we were in Europe that would happen and it would all be there when I returned. As this is true, I hadn't a byte to stand on. Still, I think it was cruel of her to make me go cold turkey. This reminds me of what it was like when I quit smoking so many years ago. I kept thinking then too that there was something I'd forgotten to do. Now that I know it's only the computer blues, I put on my layers of clothes and venture outside.

This is a cold day. Winds roar from the Sound and hit me across the face like a snapped towel. The Jeep starts right away. I pull out and head for the end of the street where I turn right, cross Sound Avenue, and take a right on the North Road. Jean Ashton lives in Millquogue, which is several towns west of Hallockville.

Why do I feel it's going to snow? Is it the metallic look of the sky or the weather report on my radio that tells me to expect it? The highway is practically empty. Along this route there's a lot of farmland and some vineyards. Also large houses I'm sure were built when this was a dirt road or no road at all. About half a mile along I see a sign announcing something called PUNKINVILLE. There's a house, a closed farm stand, and the property is littered with carved pumpkin faces.

The road narrows into two lanes as I pass a brick complex that looks newly built, but I can't tell what it is. After a marker for Pequash, I pass the town dump. And beyond the Millquogue sign I spot the landmarks Ashton has given me, and I slow down a few yards before a closed vegetable stand called Hart's. It's a dirt road with five names on separate wooden signs, one of them Ashton.

I take the turn. On either side of the road is empty land that stretches on for about six million miles. There are no houses or buildings and the trees are bare and wicked-looking. The road is unpaved, full of lumps and bumps, but the Jeep takes them without a whimper. I reach the place where the road curves to the right, and, as instructed, I continue straight ahead on what becomes a blacktop.

In moments an imposing gray and white house appears, a circular drive in front. When I get out I'm struck by the majesty of the spot, the beauty and the isolation. I wonder if Jean lives here alone. I turn to look back at the way I've come and it occurs to me that I could be standing in nineteenth-century England. Or at any time, for that matter, on any bucolic site.

I take the three gray stairs to the front door and use the brass knocker. Jean Ashton opens up at once, as though she's been standing behind the door, waiting.

"I'm so glad you could come," she says breathlessly, and practically plucks me inside.

While she hangs up my coat I look around. The first floor is an almost open space with slight divisions between living, dining, and kitchen areas. Light pours in from the wall of windows across the back of the house, which faces the Sound.

She ushers me into the living room. I sit on a couch done in blue-and-white ticking. The view is astonishing. A long lawn leads down to a staircase and beyond that, even though we're high on a bluff, I can see the water.

"Would you like some coffee?" Jean asks.

"Is it made?"

"Yes. Let me get you some."

She goes to the kitchen where I can see her fussing with a coffeepot. The room I'm in is simply but tastefully furnished. No television, no books.

When Ashton comes back she puts a tray on the coffee table. There are two steaming mugs, one pink, one gray (without any legend printed on them), and a plate of chocolate cupcakes. How did she know?

"I made them. Threw everything in I could."

I'm not sure what this means but I intend to find out. I take a napkin and a cupcake. "Looks good," I say.

She smiles and takes one for herself. Simultaneously we bite into the cakes. There are pieces of chocolate and nuts and other things I can't identify but which are delicious. It makes me lose my nostalgia for Once Upon a Tart in SoHo. I mumble my appreciation and she nods and smiles in an almost coquettish way.

Today she wears a mauve wool dress over black tights and gray leather boots. Has she dressed for me? I take a sip of coffee. It's good. "So, how can I help you, Jean?"

"I want to hire you to find out who killed Billy."

"The man in Ridley's Woods," I confirm.

"Yes."

"Tell me about him." I take out my notebook and pen.

"We're cousins. I guess I should say *were*." A sadness washes over her face as though she's switched masks. "We grew up together in Easthead. Natives, you see."

The ferries leave for Connecticut from Easthead, the town at the tip of the Fork, and I know from what the Js learned while house-hunting that it's mostly populated by those with old names and old money.

"Our families go way back. His mother is my mother's sister. They're Dormans."

She says the name as if it should tell me everything I need to know. And if I were a local, it probably would.

"Both of them, my mother and her sister, married outsiders." She gives a wry laugh. "I should talk."

"You married an outsider?"

"Yes. But I didn't consider it a bad thing the way they did in those days."

"And now you do? You said *didn't*."

"No, it's not that." She looks down, fusses with her skirt.

"What is it, then?"

"Is my marriage important to this investigation?" she asks in a neutral tone.

"No. You're important, that's all. I was wondering if you were married and now I know you are. How long have you been married to . . . what's his name?"

"Tom. Twenty-nine years. Both our children are grown and on their own. We'll be having our thirtieth wedding anniversary next fall. Sometimes I think it's unnatural."

"What is?"

"For two people to be together so long. Things get . . . oh, I don't know what I'm talking about."

Tom has probably told her for years that she doesn't know what she's talking about.

"Of course you do," I say. "It's interesting to me."

"It is?" she says, as though no one has ever been interested in anything she's had to say.

"Yes." I hope she doesn't ask why, suspect she won't because she'd view it as unmannerly. "Go on."

"Well, there are so many things that happen during those years, so many unspoken hurts and slights. Not to mention the sheer knowledge of the other person, the predictableness of it all. How can two people keep things fresh or interesting that long? I don't think it's possible."

My mind goes immediately to Alex. Was that what it was about?

"My parents were married almost forty years before my father died. And when he did she appeared more liberated than bereaved. I guess that's when I first started thinking about it."

"Did she marry again? Your mother?"

"Unfortunately she died a year later."

"Sorry."

"Oh, well," she says absently. "Tom's away a lot. Like now. He goes on business trips. He has his own advertising agency. I have to admit, I like it when I'm here alone. Do you think that's terrible?"

"No, not at all." I wonder if she has affairs.

"Well, we've gotten way off the subject. Anyway, Jane, my aunt, married John Moffat. He was working here one summer and it was supposed to be one of those hot-weather romances, if you know what I mean. But John stayed and one thing led to another and Jane married him."

"Are they still living?"

"Oh, yes. They're in Easthead."

"You'll have to give me their address."

"Naturally. Anyway, they had two children. One of them was Billy." She takes another bite of her cupcake, chews mechanically. "He and I were the same age so we were close. At least until we were fourteen or so."

"What happened then?"

"Oh, you know how these things go. Billy got interested in girls and didn't want his cousin around. But, later, when we were grown and married ourselves, we got close again."

"So Billy was married?" I remember a reference in the deli to Toby and the kid.

"Yes. A lovely girl, poor thing."

"Poor thing? You mean because of Billy's death?"

"That too, of course. But they lost a child and she never got over it. Not that Billy did, but he was able to function better. Toby . . . well, maybe mothers take these things harder. I know I'd be devastated if anything happened to either of my two." She gazes out the window for a moment then looks back at me. "You're writing all this down?" she asks, alarmed.

"I like to take notes," I explain. "Does it bother you?"

"No. I . . . Well, I hope you won't tell anyone who hired you?"

"I never do. That's confidential. But I'm curious, why not?"

"Other family members might not approve," she whispers, as if those same family members were hiding in a closet. "Tom in particular."

I guess this is because of the reputation private investigators have and nod to show I understand.

"Do the others think Billy killed himself?"

"Absolutely not. But the family doesn't like to make a fuss."

"I think what you're saying is that I should be . . . delicate . . . when I question the others?"

She breaks into a full smile. "Exactly."

"Fine. Now tell me why you think Billy was murdered."

"Can we come at it a different way?"

"Any way you'd like."

"I *know* he wouldn't kill himself. We talked about these things. When Freddy, their child, died, Billy and I talked long hours into the night. He knew he had responsibilities, especially to Toby and Lita, their other child, and even though at that point there were times when he didn't feel like going on, he knew he had to. And he thought suicide was cowardly. But if he was ever going to kill himself, it would've been then."

"You mentioned that his wife hasn't recovered as well as he had. Maybe she was a burden to him."

"I'm not going to pretend that Toby isn't difficult, but that didn't get to Billy. Of course he would've preferred that she reconcile herself to things as they were, but no matter how she behaved, he stood by her."

"Behaved?"

"Well, Toby drinks a little too much now and then."

I'm familiar with this euphemism. "A little too much"

usually means the person's a drunk. I'm also accustomed to them. My mother's a drunk although she's in total denial about it. I don't look forward to interviewing Toby.

"Jean, I think I can understand why you don't believe your cousin killed himself. But you haven't given me a reason why he might have been murdered."

"Fast food," she says.

"I beg your pardon?"

"You may have noticed that there aren't any fast-food places beyond Riverhead. The 7-Elevens are eyesores, as it is. I'm sure you won't believe this but there are people who want to bring Burger King to our Fork."

I feel she expects me to gasp but I can't manage it.

"And we all know what will follow if we let in a Burger King. Soon there'll be a Pizza Hut, a Taco Bell, a . . . a Roy Rogers, for God's sake."

No, not that, not a Roy Rogers, I want to scream, but I know this is serious stuff to Jean Ashton and others. Obviously, to Billy. "I take it your cousin felt as you do about this?"

"Absolutely. In fact, he headed AFF."

"AFF?"

"The anti–fast-food group. We call ourselves AFF."

"I see. Jean, you're not suggesting that the Burger King people. . . ."

"Oh, no, certainly not. I'm suggesting that maybe FEAG had something to do with his death. Some person or persons connected to FEAG."

FEAG. I try to guess. For Eating and Gorging? Never. I ask.

"For Expansion and Growth," Jean defines.

Of course. "What would killing Billy accomplish for the FEAG people?"

"Scare tactics."

"Murdering someone is a pretty drastic scare tactic."

"People kill each other for parking places these days. And that's another thing."

"What's another thing?"

"If we start getting fast-food places in here there'll be hostage-taking and murder after murder."

"There will?" I'm in the dark here.

"Haven't you noticed that disgruntled employees from these places are always taking hostages and killing customers?"

It's true that between fast-food joints and post offices the murder rate has risen. Still. "Well, I don't think that that necessarily —"

"It's important that you know that the FEAG people are horrible. Money-grubbing swine." Her face twists into an angry snarl, turns red.

"And who's the head of FEAG?"

"Jim Rendel." She spits out his name as if it were a caustic in her mouth.

I ask for his address. "So you think it's possible that a person or persons abducted your cousin and then hung him in Ridley's Woods because FEAG wants fast food on this Fork and wanted to scare off the AFF people."

She slowly nods, looks at me as though I've been a dull student who's finally gotten the equation. "Exactly."

I don't tell her I think it's a pretty wild idea. She's my employer and at the moment her theory is the only game on the Fork.

Five

Jean Ashton watched through the paned window next to the door, but kept out of sight. She wondered if hiring this girl was the right thing to do. What would Billy have thought? He wouldn't have objected to her engaging a private investigator, but this little thing?

She watched as the Jeep pulled out, and then went back into the living room to clear away the dishes. Involuntarily she raised her eyebrows when she noticed that all the cupcakes were gone. She couldn't remember eating more than one herself.

In the kitchen she put everything into the dishwasher and stood looking out at the water. Perhaps she hadn't told the detective enough. She recalled her last conversation with Billy. They were standing right here, he with a cup of coffee in his hand.

"I don't know, Jean. I can't explain it. I feel uneasy about everything."

He looked drawn, as though he wasn't getting enough sleep. "Can't you be more specific? Is it Toby?"

Running a hand through his thinning hair, he said, "Maybe. Maybe that's all it is."

Jean knew about Alison but Billy didn't know that; they'd never discussed it. There were some things even family didn't tell each other. At least not this family. "Is it her drinking?"

"You know, Jean, it's funny. Toby's cut back on that. But she's still so remote. Freddy's death . . . well, God, it almost killed me but you have to go on. Toby's given up."

"That's us, Billy. Our background. Go on, no matter what."

"Yes. I remember how Mother was when George died."

Jean remembered too. George had died of spinal meningitis when she and Billy were eight and George was ten. Aunt Jane played at her bridge club the day after they buried George, and went on with her life as she always had, doing the same things, never shedding a tear after those first days following her son's death.

"Toby's not like Mother." Billy added, "Thank God."

Jean smiled at him. He'd always been so handsome but the dark circles under his blue eyes gave him a haunted look now.

"Do you realize how crazy our families are, what an unnatural childhood we had?"

This startled Jean because she'd never thought of her family like this. "What do you mean?"

"Jean, for God's sake, we never talked about anything."

"That's not true," she said defensively.

"Yes, it *is* true. Sure, politics and books, but never feelings."

"That's generational."

"No. Other people talked about feelings, other people our parents' ages."

She knew that he was right. But if he felt this way why didn't he tell her about Alison? "Well, you and I have always talked."

He stepped closer to her, put his hand with its attenuated fingers on her cheek. "And I'm so grateful for that, Jean."

So why didn't she bring up the Alison matter? No. That was up to him. "Me too. So, what's this uneasy feeling you have?"

"I think I'm being followed."

*   *   *

Damn, Jean thought now. Why hadn't she told the detective that? Stupid. How could she have forgotten something so important? Was it because at the time she didn't quite believe him, thought he was overtired, and put it out of her mind? Or was it that background again, coming to the fore even though she'd hired a private investigator? That substratum, the nub in her marrow, that refused to tell all, even if that was the point. The Dorman blood raced through her and she'd be loyal to the end. Well, no. She'd call the Laurano girl and tell her about Billy's fear of being followed. She'd do it the second she got back from having her hair done. And that was final.

Six

Jim Rendel, the head of FEAG, is a lawyer with an office in Seaview. I take Route 25 back because I want to get a better look at the village centers. Pequash is the first after Millquogue. It's not much of a place: a library, drugstore, antiques, cute diner, a pet shop (which surprises me), and a deli that has a sign in the window advertising homemade waffles. I make a mental note of this. There are a few other stores but the light changes and I continue on.

Little Bay is next but there's no real town. Eventually I come to Hallockville. It has a small shopping center called Plume Hill. A lot of stores are listed on a sign between the enter and exit drives. On the main street there's a bank, drugstore, clothing stores, and other businesses. Further on there's a video store, and the ubiquitous 7-Eleven.

Various restaurants and stores dot the landscape for a while longer. After that, a few houses and a closed information center. I slow to thirty at the approach into Seaview, where I pass a school on one side and houses and a church on the other. As I noticed yesterday, when we went shopping for cleaning supplies, the village center has a four-screen movie theater. Only now do I realize that Seaview is larger than any of the other hamlets I've been through. I spot a sign for Rendel's office and park across the street from it.

Inside, I find that he's on the second floor so I climb the carpeted stairs. A young woman in a cable-knit sweater sits behind a small white desk. I say hello and she smiles back at me. She doesn't have a nameplate.

"Is Jim Rendel here?"

"Sure."

"Could I see him?"

"Is there something I could help you with?"

"What's your name?"

"Betty Fitzpatrick."

"Well, Ms. Fitzpatrick, you can't help me because I need to talk to Mr. Rendel."

"What about?"

I'm surprised at this direct questioning. "It's a private matter."

She looks as though I've slapped her; her small mouth purses. "He'll ask," she states reasonably.

I reach in my bag, take out a business card, and hand it to her.

"Get real," she says, smiling, looking from the card to me.

I don't believe this. "I am real, that's real."

"A private investigator? You?"

Why must I always go through this? Is it because I'm a woman, because I'm short, what? "Yes, me."

"Really?"

"Yes."

She stares at the card as though it will tell her how I could actually be a P.I. "It says New York City."

"I know."

"Is it legal for you to be investigating out of your jurisdiction?"

God, I hate TV cop shows. "I don't have a jurisdiction. Could you please give that to Mr. Rendel."

"He's not going to believe this one," she mumbles as she walks away.

While I wait, I try practicing my upside-down-reading skills. The problem is, the document on her desk is in legalese and I probably couldn't understand it right side up.

Ms. Fitzpatrick returns. "He wants to know what it's about," she says superciliously.

"William Moffat."

This time when she returns she says, "He'll see you."

Now it's my turn to be scornful but I'm not. "Thanks."

She makes a grudging sound, then opens the gate in the counter and I follow her to the back. Rendel is on the phone and motions me to a straight-back chair in front of his desk.

I take the seat and look around. The inevitable family photo graces the top of a small bookcase. It's obviously not current because in it Rendel looks twenty-five years younger. There are three children and they are small. The woman, his wife, I presume, is blond and permed, a stiff smile stuck on her pretty face. The clothes are definitely seventies style.

The room is what I've come to call "the lawyer-room," which is furnished with heavy dark pieces, chairs of hunter green leather, and the obligatory set of law books on the shelves.

Rendel replaces the handset in its cradle, rises, and reaches across the desk to shake my hand, envelops it as though what I offer is puny, which it is by comparison.

He reseats himself. "So, Laurie, how can I help?"

I resent him calling me by what he thinks is my first name.

"Lauren."

"Sorry."

Rendel's a large man with a flat stomach for someone his age, middle to late fifties. His hair is brown, almost the color of mine but his has less gray in it. He styles it simply, short and parted on the right. His brown eyes are my color too but they have a sad look, maybe depressed. It's not a handsome face but it isn't ugly either. *Ordinary* is the word that comes to mind. He's dressed in a blue suit with a white shirt and a rep tie.

"You're investigating Moffat's suicide?"

"My client doesn't think it was suicide."

He raises two bushy eyebrows. "What, then?"

"Murder."

"Murder? Funny way to murder somebody. I mean, there's easier ways."

"Like what?" I ask seriously.

Rendel chuckles. "Well, you know what I mean. Who's gonna hang a man to murder him when there's guns and knives and such?"

"Somebody who wants it to look like suicide."

"Guess you have a point there."

"You knew Mr. Moffat, didn't you?"

"Yes."

"Did you like him?"

He shrugs. "Didn't feel one way or the other."

"But he opposed you in the fast-food argument."

"Yes, he did. But I wouldn't kill him because of that."

"I didn't say you did."

"But that's what you're driving at."

"Am I?"

He looks at his watch. "What is it you want? I'm a busy man, Laurie."

I don't bother to correct him because he already knows. This is a common tactic to throw off the interviewer.

"How long did you know Mr. Moffat?"

"Maybe thirty years, maybe less."

"When's the last time you saw him alive?"

"At a meeting. A FEAG meeting. Know what that is?"

I nod. "How long ago was the meeting?"

He scrunches his eyebrows together to suggest that he's thinking.

"Better look at my calendar." He rustles through a flat appointment book. "Here it is. The last FEAG meeting was two weeks ago."

"And you didn't see him after that?"

"Not that I recall."

"Was that usual?"

"I guess. Never thought about it. But our paths seldom crossed."

I move to another area. "You know Jean Ashton?"

He rolls his eyes heavenward. "Yes, I know that loony tunes."

"Why do you call her that?"

"Because that's what she is. A nut case, a lunatic. That who you're working for?"

"You know I can't tell you who my employer is. In your opinion, why is Jean Ashton crazy?" I can't help thinking about her outburst on fast-food places and murder.

"Always on her hobby horse about one thing or another. Troublemaker."

"And she opposes FEAG?"

"Stupid woman. I don't know what's wrong with these people. Progress is what it's all about."

How I would like to have a nickel for every horror executed in the name of progress.

"Do you have any ideas who might have wanted Moffat dead?"

"Can't say that I do. 'Course there's always *cherchez la femme,* as they say."

"Oh? Did Moffat have a woman friend?"

"He had a wife."

"Why do I feel you didn't mean her?"

"You're smart for a girl."

I count to ten.

"He had a wife *and* a girlfriend. Probably both wouldn't have minded seeing him dead."

"Why?"

"They knew about each other. Well, naturally Alison knew about Toby, Bill's wife. But Toby knew about Alison, too. Hell, everybody knows about her."

I wonder if Jean knows and if so why she didn't tell me. "Could you give me her full name and address?"

"Why not?" Rendel takes a pink file card from a box on his desk, writes on it.

"I suppose you have an alibi for Moffat's time of death?"

"Don't know if I do or not. What was the time of death?"

He's sharp. I try an end run. "Where were you last night?"

"I was home with my wife. You want to ask her, I'll give you my address. Her name's Tina."

I know this would be a waste of time. From the photograph I can tell that Tina Rendel is a doormat type and would do whatever her husband asked, including lie if he murdered someone.

He hands me the file card. It says: Alison Von Elder, 123 Queen Street, Easthead.

"Do you happen to know if Ms. Von Elder works?"

"I think she does. I can't remember where right now."

"So she might not be at home at this hour?"

"Might not. 'Course, she might be in mourning." Something about this statement makes Rendel grin and he shows small sharp teeth.

"Thanks. You've been very helpful." I take out one of my cards, cross out the number, and write the one in Hallockville. "In case you think of anything else."

He takes it from me as though it's contaminated. "I won't think of anything," he says.

"You never know."

"I know."

What's the use?

Outside it hasn't gotten any warmer. Against the wind I pull up the collar of my trusty blue Eddie Bauer jacket. When I look at the card Rendel gave me I swear at myself for not getting directions. I know how to get to Easthead but where the hell is Queen Street? Oh, well, how hard can it be to find?

Seven

Jim Rendel felt like breaking a few heads. What the hell was this now? What dodo got this bitch involved in something local, something they could take care of themselves? Well, why the fuck was he asking himself that? He knew it was Ashton. Crazy bitch.

He stared at the photo on his desk and thought about his wife. They were all alike. His eyes skidded off his sons, who, as far as he was concerned, had all turned out like their mother. Stupid and useless.

Anyway, no time for that now. What was he going to do about this interloper, this big-city dumb detective? The last thing FEAG needed was shit like this. And what if this girl found out that Bill Moffat had been in his office two days before he died? Sat right across from him, his face all red and scrunched up like he might explode.

"Listen, Jim, you people aren't going to win this one so why don't you let it go?" Moffat said.

Jim tipped back his chair, his tasseled loafers making taps on the floor beneath the desk. "What are you getting all worked up about, Billy?"

"Don't call me Billy. That's reserved for my family."

"What should I call you then? Mr. Moffat?" He laughed.

"I want to know why you're having me followed."

Jim came forward in the chair with a thud, leaned on the desk. "What the fuck are you talking about?"

"Don't play dumb with me, Rendel. Somebody's been fol- lowing me for the last week. And they stink at it, too, because I spotted them right away. Always at night so I can't get a good look, but I know you have someone out there."

"You're a crazy bastard, Moffat. Now get the hell outta my office."

"Not until you promise to call off your watchdog."

"I'm telling you I don't know what you're talking about."

"The people don't want a Burger King here and having me followed isn't going to change anything. You think you're going to win this thing with scare tactics but it isn't going to work. You can have a militia follow me and that's not going to stop AFF. Besides, I know some other things, too."

"What's that supposed to mean?" Jim sneered. "What other things?"

"I think you know. I can't prove anything yet, Rendel, but I will. And when I do, you and all of your group are going to pay, no matter how high up this goes."

"You sound like a lunatic," Jim said. "I have no idea what you're referring to. You come in here accusing me of every- thing under the sun. I think you've lost it, Moffat. What other things?"

"I'm almost there, Rendel. Just a few more pieces."

"You're crazy. I don't have any idea what you mean. Now get out of my office before I call the police."

Jim didn't want that Big Apple gumshoe here looking into God knew what, even if she was a stupid girl. Well, maybe getting her on to Moffat's girlfriend would keep her busy.

He felt a chill; a goose walking over his grave, his mother would've said. *You and all of your group are going to pay.*

There were two things he needed to do right away. He had to talk to his secretary and instruct her not to mention Moffat's visit, and he had to call the chief of police. He picked up the phone.

Eight

Since I'm so close by, the thought of visiting the Js' work site crosses my mind. But why fuel Kip's resentment of my not helping out, working on a crime case instead? No. I reject the idea as though it were covered in mold.

Instead, I drive to the end of Main Street, see the water to my right so I take a left and go through more of the residential part of town. There are some big beautiful houses here and I suspect they were once owned by the affluent. But now this is probably a busy artery, especially in summer, and the rich wouldn't want to live here.

Eventually I hit the North Road and turn right toward Easthead. I wonder if Ms. Von Elder is one of the cream of the crop who lives there.

After passing a sign that informs me I'm in Bay Haven I cross a stretch of highway with water on either side, and then another sign announces Easthead. To my left I see huge rambling old houses on a cliff. I assume they overlook the Sound. Farther along on my right, I spot a store called the Candy Maker. Oh, no. Oh, yes.

I see in my rearview mirror that no one's behind me so I make a squealing reckless right and pull into the parking area in front of the store.

It's a small red building. I enter. Oh, happiness. There's nothing like this smell. Although the store has other candy it's mostly filled with all forms, shapes, and types of chocolate, the aroma permeating everything.

An average-size woman in her fifties approaches me. Her red hair piled high brings the Leaning Tower of Pisa to mind.

"May I help you, dear?" She speaks with a slight, indeterminate accent.

Help is what I need but not the kind she means. Display cases line the room and on top of the counters are large glass crocks filled with broken bits of chocolate. The shelves on the walls are crowded with jars of chocolate-covered everything.

"I'll look for now," I say, as though I were in Tiffany's. As I move along peering into the cases, registering milk, white, dark, I feel the woman's eyes on me. I stop in front of a section marked NON-SUGAR, amazed as always that anyone would buy such a thing. It's like alcoholics drinking non-alcoholic beer. What's the point?

"You have to be careful with those, dear," the woman warns.

I turn to face her. "Careful?"

"The diet ones, sugarless." She purses her lips in a prissy pout.

I still don't understand and say so.

"Sorbitol," she says succinctly.

"Sorbitol?"

"You eat too much, then putt, putt, putt." She bends over pointing her ass in my direction, her finger illustrating the passageway of the putts. When she stands up she gives a wide grin, then laughs hysterically.

I try to smile but I know it isn't convincing. You have to admit this is embarrassing. I quickly realize that if it were happening in New York I wouldn't think twice about it.

"You know what I mean?" she asks. "Putt, putt?"

"Yes, sure."

"Sorbitol."

"Right. Sorbitol."

"They fly people to the moon but they cannot make a sugarless candy that won't make you putt, putt." She leans over and again points to her ass. I begin to think she might be a fetishist or something. Why else would she keep doing this?

"Putt, putt."

I want to get off this topic now. "I'll have some of those over there." I indicate the case with real sugared chocolate, the round ones filled with a pink cream.

She stands up, follows the direction of my finger. "How much, dear?"

"Show me what a quarter of a pound looks like."

The stare she gives me lets me know that it's not many and that I'm a piker. "Half a pound," I amend, and wonder why I'm concerned with what this woman thinks of me. Will I ever get over this? I must immediately start ignoring what others think about what I do, who I am.

"I'm happy you didn't pick the sorbitol ones."

Oh no. I'm afraid now she'll find a way to tell me that these *don't* make you putt, putt. So while she fills my order I ask her for directions to 123 Queen Street. She gives them, then we exchange money and candy.

"You must have a piece," she says.

I don't need a second invitation. I open the little white bag, dip in, and pull out a milk chocolate cream, bite it in half. Heaven. "The best," I say.

She walks me to the door, smiles brilliantly, which I receive as her approval, and I care.

A large monument in the shape of an obelisk heralds the entrance to the town of Easthead. It's picture-postcard time. Some of the houses on this main street are seventeenth-century; none are contemporary. The town boasts a post office and a general store. At the end, the street curves and you see the Sound. It's easy to imagine what this spot must've been like in the sixteen and seventeen hundreds.

Several blocks along is Queen Street. I make a left, which is the only way I can turn. Number 123 is an old farmhouse set back from the road. I pull into the drive, pop another candy, savor it, leave the bag (what if Von Elder wants some?), then get out of the Jeep.

The house looks in need of TLC. Definitely a paint job. When I go up the five steps I feel them sag. The porch floor squeaks and groans as I cross to the door. There doesn't appear to be a bell so I knock on the glass and pray it doesn't break.

I can see into the house. There's a small living room with stairs coming into it. The white wicker furniture has blue pillows. To the left is a TV set. A filled bookcase is against one wall. Past that is a doorway which I guess is to the kitchen.

This time I knock with slightly more force. A woman in a ruby-colored robe and matching slippers comes from that direction. She walks with a hesitant step, almost a shuffle. But as she gets nearer I can see she's quite a bit younger than her demeanor indicates.

She clutches the neck of her robe tighter around her and looks at me through the glass.

"Ms. Von Elder?" I shout.

She nods.

"May I talk to you?"

Through the glass, muffled but intelligible, she asks who I am. I take out my wallet and hold my P.I. license up to the glass.

Von Elder leans forward, squints, then looks back at me, says nothing.

"I'd like to talk about Bill Moffat."

A clear flash of pain crosses her face. After a few moments of deliberation she opens the door and steps aside for me to enter.

"Thanks so much," I say, hurrying in so she can close the door against the cold air.

Now that I'm inside I can tell that the walls are paneled and have been painted white.

"Let's go in the kitchen. I'm having coffee. Would you like some?"

"Yes, sure. Thanks." I follow her into a typically large farmhouse kitchen, a round oak table in the center. She tells me to sit while she gets a mug for me and pours the coffee. There's milk and Sweet 'N Low on the table. When she sets the mug in front of me I see that it says MOM on it and it makes me wonder.

"You have children?"

"Children?"

I indicate the mug.

She smiles, which changes her face from conventional to beautiful. "Yard sale."

"It's apt that you gave me this one," I say. "Means, opportunity, motive." I grin but it quickly fades as I register the blank look on her face. "For a crime. 'M.O.M.' is short for 'means, opportunity, motive.' It's M.M.O. but it could be M.O.M."

"Yes, I know what M.M.O. means."

So why, I wonder, did she have me go through that whole explanation.

Alison Von Elder is a marvelous-looking woman. She has wavy ash blond hair to her shoulders, deep blue eyes, a straight classic nose, and full lips with a slight parenthesis at each corner.

"Do you know why I'm here?"

"You said to talk with me about Bill. The police have already been here but you're private so I'd guess someone hired you."

I put a packet of sweetener and a shot of milk into my coffee. When she takes a swallow of hers I notice the mug says OLDEST LIVING LAWYER. Not only is this not true, even if she is a lawyer, it suddenly seems like mugs are taking over where T-shirts leave off.

"Yes, someone did hire me."

"Probably his wife."

"I can't reveal who my client is, Ms. Von Elder."

"Call me Alison. And I know the drill."

I wonder how she knows but suspect it's like everyone else: television and novels, most of which get everything wrong. "You were a close friend of Bill's, weren't you?"

She laughs, deep and honeyed. "You into euphemisms?"

I feel a bit foolish. "Okay, you were his lover?"

"Yes." She looks as if she might cry.

"For how long?"

"The last two years. In the beginning I thought he'd leave his wife, but after the first year I knew that wasn't going to happen. I was twenty-eight then and I had to make a decision. Did I want a full life with husband and children, or half a life and no children? You're thinking, who would choose the latter, aren't you?"

"Yes, I suppose I am."

"The thing is, I loved Bill and I couldn't imagine life without him in some form. Now he's dead, I'm thirty and have nothing."

"But you were content before he died?"

"Died? Murdered is more like it, isn't it?"

"Why do you say that?"

"Someone must think he was murdered or you wouldn't be investigating. Besides, he'd never kill himself. Bill loved life even though sometimes he felt guilty about our relationship."

"Do *you* think he was murdered?"

"Yes. Aside from anything else, he was too responsible. He wouldn't leave Toby to deal with Lita by herself."

"Lita?"

"Their daughter. She's autistic."

I wonder why Jean didn't tell me this. Not that I believed it had any relevance to Moffat's alleged murder. But it was the kind of thing that would normally be mentioned as background info.

"Was Lita's autism why Bill wouldn't leave his wife?"

"Mainly."

"So if he wouldn't leave her for that reason, he'd hardly kill himself," I say.

"Exactly." She takes a gentle sip of her coffee.

"Any ideas who might want him dead?"

"I've been thinking about that. I can't conjure up a single

enemy. Of course there are the FEAG people. Do you know about them?"

"Yes, I do."

"But it seems so unlikely for anyone to kill someone over a fast-food establishment."

"There have been stranger motives for murder, believe me."

"You mean like the Cheerleader Mom murder?" She runs a manicured hand through her blond hair.

"Well, yes, like that."

"I read a lot of true crime. Do you?"

"Read true crime? I used to when there wasn't so much of it."

"I know what you mean. A lot of it's trash but there are the good ones, like the books Jack Olson writes."

"Yes, he's good." I don't give this preoccupation too much import because half the world reads true crime these days; so many people that bookstores devote whole sections to it. Anyway, it explains why she's conversant with police jargon.

"Is there anyone else who might want Bill dead?"

"Other than those FEAG people I think you'll find Bill was a well-liked guy."

"What about you?" I ask her directly.

"Me?"

"Maybe you were fed up, angry. Who could blame you?"

She laughs. "Anyone could blame me. I made my bed, so to speak. And what would I gain?"

"I guess we'll know when the will is read."

"Ms. Laurano, I resent that." Her eyes take on a darker shade of blue.

"Call me Lauren. I can understand why you'd resent it but everyone is under suspicion for now."

"Well, Lauren, I think when the will is read you'll find that I'm not mentioned. Bill would never embarrass his family by leaving me anything, and I happen to have a good job."

"What do you do?"

"I work with autistic children. I couldn't go in today."

"Understandable."

"I hate to let the children down. But I wouldn't have been any good to them." Her face flushes and the eyes fill.

"Is that how you met Bill? Teaching Lita?"

"Yes. And Toby."

"What do you think of Toby?"

"Am I the best person to ask?"

"You're the best person to ask about what *you* think."

"That's true." Alison takes a deep breath. "I think she's a manipulative, selfish bitch."

"That nice, huh?"

She smiles. "Ask someone with a less biased view."

"I will."

"I bet some will give you the same reaction."

"One thing I've learned since I've been in this business, Alison, is that there are as many different views of a person as there are people with opinions. But you're right, there will be others who'll have the same take on Toby you do. Do you think she'd kill her husband?"

"What for? She needed him around."

"Maybe she found out about you."

"She's known about me practically from the beginning."

"And didn't care?"

"Was off the hook."

I give her a quizzical look.

"The sex hook."

"Ah. They didn't have an active sex life, then?"

"You could say that, yes," Alison says sarcastically.

"Do you think Toby was seeing anyone else?"

"Very, very doubtful. I don't think she likes sex, Lauren. Don't think she ever did."

"I'll leave you my number and if you think of anything else let me know."

She pushes a pad and pen toward me.

As we walk to the door, Alison says, "I hope you catch the bastard."

"I'll try," I say.

We shake hands and I admire her grip. So rare in any generation under mine.

Nine

Alison went upstairs the minute the detective left. She was curious about her, what made her go into that line of work. For one thing, she was so short. Alison could have kicked herself for mentioning her true-crime reading. What if Laurano started thinking something about that?

She stopped abruptly at the door to her bedroom. She could see the end of the unmade bed and her heart gave a lurch of pain. Stepping into the room the whole bed came into view. Slowly she moved to it, sat down near the head. She reached out a hand and touched the pillow he always used. Would it have made any difference if the last time he was here she'd known it was the last time? You never know that about sex, or usually you don't. She certainly hadn't. And it was less than a week ago.

"Sometimes," Bill said as they had their post-sex cigarette, "I think Toby would like me dead."

Alison pushed his hair off his brow. "Why do you say that?"

"I don't know. The way she looks at me, I guess."

"Why doesn't she give you a divorce?"

"Family."

"Yes, I know. There've never been any divorces in the Latham clan."

"Well, it makes sense to her. And then there's Lita."

Alison nodded, understanding that completely. "Well, I'm

sure she doesn't wish you dead, Bill. Who'd help her with Lita then?"

"True. But there are some who wish me dead. I'm getting too close to certain stuff."

"What stuff?"

"I can't tell you."

She sat partway up. "Are you kidding? I thought you told me everything."

"I do. But it's better if you don't know about this . . . at least right now."

"FEAG business?"

He didn't answer, blew a plume of smoke above him.

"Bill?"

"Let's change the subject."

"It's not, is it? It's something else. What?"

"Not now, Alison."

Oh, why hadn't he told her? She was convinced whatever it was had something to do with his death, his murder. And why hadn't she told the police or that detective what he'd said? Well, that was an easy one to answer: She couldn't let the detective or the police know how much she knew. If she did, if she got more involved than she already was, they might start looking into her background, and then where would she be? Maybe in jail again.

Ten

It's time for lunch. I could join the others at the Js' house but I decide it will be more fruitful to go into a local eatery. One never knows what one might pick up . . . hopefully not food poisoning.

There's nowhere to eat in Easthead and a place on the North Road called the Hellenic is closed for the winter, so I drive into Seaview, where I find the Paradise Café on the main street. From the outside the Paradise looks like it hasn't been renovated since it was built, probably in the thirties. I like that. After I park and get out I start to lock up, then laugh at myself for my New York City paranoia and put the keys away.

The Paradise is exactly as I'd imagined. Wooden booths, art deco mirrors on the wainscotted walls, a long lunch counter with stools that appear to have real red leather seats.

Not.

Some fool has completely redone the place, making it look like any coffee shop you might find in N.Y.C. No booths, plastic-top tables, Sheetrock walls, and synthetic green for the stool seats. Why? Is this what people want?

Normally I'd take a table but today I sit at the counter, the better to overhear things.

To my immediate right sits a man wearing a worn, blue woolen suit jacket and when he reaches for the salt I see the unmistakable flash of a gun in a holster. Are the citizens armed? Maybe I should have locked the car.

I pull myself together, realizing how many people carry guns in New York City. Still, it gives me pause to think that this kind of madness has reached the end of Long Island.

To my left is another man whom some would call "a man of size." I call him obese. In front of him is a cup of coffee, one boiled egg, and unbuttered toast. Who does he think he's fooling?

As I mull this over I hear a crackling sound that comes from my countermate to my right.

He reaches into his pocket and pulls out a two-way radio. A tinny voice says, "Charlie one to Charlie two."

Blue jacket pushes a button on his device and answers, "Charlie two here, what's up?"

"Eight-nine-four-five. Another one. Same story. Address: fourteen twenty-one Sixth Street, Seaview."

"Right. Over and out." He shuts off his radio, shoves it into his pocket, gets off the stool. "Later," he says to the counterman, grabs a heavy coat from the rack, and goes out the door.

I'm right behind him. Now I know he's a cop. What does it mean, *another one?* I don't know the codes they use here so it could be almost anything. I guess it's a break-in, but I can't be sure.

His tan Chevy is parked across the street from my Jeep and he starts up as I get in, saluting myself for not locking. He takes off and I do a U and follow. He goes straight on Main. After a few blocks he turns onto Sixth Street. We go over the railroad tracks, pass a couple of cross streets, and he pulls up in front of a large gray Victorian house where several police cars and an ambulance are parked, all their lights flashing. I drive by and stop three houses past. It's hard to disguise what you're doing in a small town.

I stay in my car and watch the action through my rearview mirror. All personnel seem to be inside except for one uniformed cop at the door. If it was a break-in, then someone was home and got hurt, or there wouldn't be an ambulance in front.

A loud thump on my window makes me jump six miles

in my seat and hit my head on the roof. When I look, I see a man in a blue-billed cap. I turn the key and power down the window.

"Whatcha doin' here?"

"You scared me," I accuse, practicing the best defense: offense.

"License and registration," he says.

My strategy hasn't worked. "Why?"

He touches a yellow-gloved hand to the bill of his cap, pushes it farther down over his narrow forehead, squints his eyes. "Because I said."

"Who are you?" I ask, innocently.

He sighs, reaches into his inside pocket, pulls out a brown leather snap case, and shows me his shield. I read his name: Jay Mills.

"Oh. Okay, Detective Mills." I dig into my bag, take out my wallet, remove the things he's requested, and hand them to him. It's cold with the window open and I wish he'd hurry.

He's a tall, lanky man with wisps of red hair peeking from under his hat. Freckles cover his cheeks and the bridge of a long nose.

"Didn't think you were a local," he says, as though I'm filth. "What're you doing here?"

"Here? You mean on this Fork?"

He turns his head to the side, signaling disgust, then looks back at me. "On this street."

There's no use making something up. "I wanted to see what was going on."

"You're kidding." He smiles.

My candor seems to disarm him.

"You come all the way from" — he looks back at my license — "Perry Street in New York to see what's goin' on on Sixth Street in Seaview, huh?"

My veracity has accomplished nothing but suspicion. "Not exactly. I'm renting a house out here."

"Well, lady, we don't need you to see what's going on, okay?"

I try another bit of honesty because I have nothing to lose.

"I'm actually a private investigator on a case and please don't laugh because it's the truth." I show him my P.I. license.

It takes him about an hour to read it. I make no comment on this.

"What case you on?"

"Moffat."

"That's no case. That was suicide."

"My employer doesn't think so. Look, can you tell me what's going on here? I know this is another one," I say slyly, as if I know what I'm talking about.

"You do, huh? Haven't had a Silk Scarf murder for a while but this seems to be the same M.O."

Oh, happiness. He believes and he tells.

"That's what I thought," I say, confidentially. I decide to take a flyer. "So that makes three, right?"

"Where you get your information? This one makes four."

Four. Four murders on the North Fork? I must get to a library immediately.

"Jesus, don't know how Sonny Kempler's gonna take this, them losin' a kid few months back."

"I didn't know that," I say, feeling genuinely sympathetic.

"Let's face it, girl, you don't know squat about nothin'."

I try my damnedest not to blush but I've never discovered the trick for achieving this. "What makes you say that, Detective Mills?" I challenge.

"Ah, hell, you city cops been out here before this, ya know."

"I'm not a cop."

"Private dick, same shit."

It's pointless to go on pretending. "Okay, you're on to me. I had no idea there'd been any murders here. I'm stunned."

"Stunned, huh?"

"Why hasn't this been given more attention . . . in the media, for instance?"

"Has. Where you been? Too much attention, you ask me. 'Course, bunch a stuff like O.J. and them others, Mendel brothers, maybe overshadowed it. In the city them Granny killings, Central Park things . . . stuff like that."

I had stopped watching anything but *MacNeil-Lehrer* on PBS for my news a few years back. Kip's rants started my drift away from the local, and, eventually, the commercial national news. All of it had become too cute, not to mention the tabloid touch tarring everything with its base brush. And though I continued to read the *New York Times* I skipped over the more sensational stuff since I had to deal with it regularly in my work. But now I could see that there were some things I wasn't getting from my ethical news sources. Still, it was odd that I'd missed this completely.

Mills says, "On the other hand, even though I said it got too much attention, you could say it was given short shrift, like the women here don't count, or somethin'." He shakes his head despairingly. "Less somethin' happens down the city or out Hollywood, any big, big place, seems like nobody cares."

"I don't think that's exactly true. Sure, big cities get more play but think of all the —"

"Hey, enough of this," he says abruptly and gives back my license and registration. "Chief'll have my head I don't get you outta here."

"Sure, I understand."

"Now you don't tell no one about this, about this bein' another one, till it's official, hear?"

"Promise."

"Me and my big mouth."

"Don't worry," I assure him.

He touches his fingers to the edge of the bill as though he's tipping his hat to me, gives the Jeep a pat, and walks away. I turn over the engine and take off.

I drive back to Hallockville, where I'd seen a library. I'm sure there's one in Seaview but I don't know where it is. I take a right into the shopping center called Plume Hill, go over two speed bumps, and wind my way around into the parking lot.

The library is a red-brick building. I walk up a ramp, open a heavy glass door into a foyer, then a second glass door. Immediately in front of me is a counter that separates the staff from the users. Signs indicate where to check out and return books.

Sitting behind the checkout area is a gray-haired woman with tidy features, glasses perched on an aristocratic nose. She wears a name tag that says EDITH.

"May I help you?"

"I'd like to look up some things in the local paper."

"The North Fork Times?"

"Yes, if that's the name of it."

She smiles and I like her immediately.

"Well, it's not the only one but it's the best one. We have it on microfiche if you'd like to use that."

I tell her that would be fine.

She asks another woman to take her place at the desk and comes out to my area. "My name is Edith."

"Yes, I know," I say.

She shakes her head, laughs quietly. "I can't get used to these name tags. An innovation by the director. Are you new here?"

"I'm visiting," I say and tell her my name.

The microfiche machine is in the reference room.

"How far back do you want to go?" she asks.

I don't know why, but I feel I can trust Edith. "When did the murders start?"

She lifts an orderly eyebrow. "Murders?"

Perhaps my trust was misplaced. "The Silk Scarf murders," I press on.

Her face pales slightly. "It's been a number of years; four."

"It worries you," I say.

"I *am* a woman, although definitely not in his age range," Edith says, perhaps with a tinge of regret, longing for youth.

"Did you know any of the victims?"

She appears startled. "Why do you ask?"

Should I tell her I'm a P.I. and that this is a standard question? I do.

"Oh, I thought. . . . Are you investigating the murders?"

"Not exactly."

"What could that possibly mean?" she says. "You are or you're not."

I couldn't agree with her more; *not exactly* is a meaningless phrase and I hate when people use it, and its cousin *not really*. "I'm sorry. I'm not officially investigating. I've been hired to look into the Moffat case but the Silk . . ." I trail off because I don't know how to explain, having promised Mills not to mention the latest murder. "I overheard someone talking in a luncheonette in Seaview," I offer, which is almost the truth.

"I see." She turns her back on me and begins to rifle through the microfiche files.

I've offended her somehow and I want to apologize. I touch her shoulder and she wheels around.

"Yes?" Her penetrating blue eyes question me as well as the one word.

"I feel . . . I'm sorry if I upset you, I didn't mean to."

She sighs; shoulders slump slightly as she backs off. "I'm sure you didn't. It was your question. It took me by surprise . . . I thought you knew and . . . Oh, I don't know what I thought."

"My question?"

"You asked if I knew any of the victims. I do. Did. One of them was my niece."

Eleven

"I'm so sorry," I tell her. And I am.

Edith waves a hand as if to say it doesn't matter, but of course it does.

She says, "Connie was the second one. She was eighteen."

I recognize a need to talk so I nod sympathetically, hoping to encourage her.

"What a lovely girl she was." Edith's eyes shine with the first trace of tears. "Not that that makes the difference. I mean, lovely or not, she didn't deserve to die . . . to be murdered. None of them did."

"When was it, Edith?"

"As I said, she was the second so it was about three and a half years ago. Connie would have been twenty-one now. The thing that makes it so awful, that makes everyone so angry, is that nothing's been done to stop this maniac."

Relatives of victims never think anything's being done unless there's an arrest. They don't understand that the investigation goes on, the leads get followed up, no matter how crazy they are. I don't know how they operate here but my guess is that it's the same as everywhere else. I don't defend the police because I'm sure this will make Edith stop talking.

"Have there been any leads?"

"Oh, yes, after every murder the police have dragged in

this one and that one . . . but it's never amounted to anything. The rest of the time . . . well, who knows what they do?"

"But they have had suspects?"

"I suppose."

"Did you know any of them?"

"Not personally. Maybe I saw them around but here's the truth: They always picked up blacks, never whites. The police can be very racist, you know."

Right. "So as far as you understand, they never questioned a white suspect."

"That's correct."

"And you, do you or did you ever have any ideas of your own as to who the perp . . . the killer might be?"

"It did occur to me that Connie's murder might be one of those copycat killings. I thought it might be her boyfriend."

"Why did you think that?"

"She was trying to break up with him and he was resisting. All the details of the first murder were in the paper . . . who knew then it was going to be a series of killings?"

"You mean the paper published the method of the killing?"

"The silk scarf . . . yes."

"Who was the first victim?"

"Her name was Marilyn Hillard. She was in her thirties."

"And that happened four years ago?"

Edith nods.

"Did you tell the police about your suspicions? That it might be Connie's boyfriend?"

"No. My sister, Connie's mother, told me to stay out of it so I did."

"And the boyfriend . . . what happened to him?"

"He's still around, the ba . . ." She trails off.

Decorum deters her from calling him a bastard.

"What's his name?"

Edith cocks her head to one side. "I thought you were investigating the Moffat death?"

"I am. But this interests me, too."

"Why?"

Good question. "Well, it sounds like you have a serial killer here and, as I'm a detective, naturally it piques my curiosity."

She winces.

"I know that sounds callous and I suppose it is in a way. But I don't mean it to be. You never know, while I'm working on the Moffat case I might come across something that will have some bearing on the Silk Scarf murders."

Edith ponders this, then says, "I suppose that's possible. Well, Connie's boyfriend's name was, is, Lee Howard. He works at Vreeland's Motors, sells cars."

"Where is Vreeland's?"

"Here. In Hallockville, on the main road going toward Pequash."

"That's west, toward New York?"

"I think of it as toward Riverhead, but yes, west."

"Thanks."

"Are you going to question him?"

I shrug because I'm not sure what I'm going to do.

"He's slippery," she cautions; her eyes show anger now.

"I'll keep that in mind. What was Connie's last name?"

"Kuerstiner. You still want to see the microfiche?"

I tell her I do and settle down to go through the documents.

Vreeland's Motors is right after the Kartalia vineyard and right before a small complex of commercial buildings that resemble a mini-mall. I pull into Vreeland's parking lot, not sure what I'm doing here. The articles about the various murders have told me little, except to give me the name of the third victim, which I could have gotten from Edith. Lee Howard was never mentioned. I know I should be concentrating on the Moffat thing but I want to see Howard. You never know.

When I enter the showroom a man in his late fifties, pleasant face, wearing a pair of glasses and the omnipresent billed cap, looks up from his desk.

"Help ya?" he asks in a soft voice.

My guess is he's too old to be Howard, then I take in the nameplate. John Vreeland. "Mr. Howard here?"

"Yep. He's in the bathroom right now. Sure I can't do anything for ya?"

"Thanks, but I need to talk to him."

"You thinking of buying?"

"Might be."

"You from the city?"

"Yes."

"Not me. Born an' bred here. This is the last good place on earth. Don't know how you people stand the dirt in there."

Before I get a chance to defend my city I see a man come out of a door across the showroom. He's tucking the last piece of his shirttail into his pants. Vreeland looks over at him.

"That's Lee."

"Thanks." I go over, stick out my hand. "Mr. Howard, I'm Lauren Laurano and you were recommended to me."

He takes my hand; his grip is soft.

"How do you do," he says. "Who was that?"

Oh, boy. I take a chance. "Stash Volinewski."

He smiles. "Oh, yeah. Sold him his last car. Have a seat."

I do. Howard looks like he's in his late twenties. He has blue eyes and blond hair combed straight back. For a man, his features are small, but regular, and he's handsome in a conventional way. He wears a green tie that picks up the color in a good flannel shirt, and brown wool pants. When he places his hands on his desk I notice that the fingers are long and delicate, the nails clean.

Although it's unnecessary, he smoothes down his hair, gives me a salesman's smile. "So what can I do for you?"

"I thought I might take a look at a Grand Cherokee Laredo."

"Outstanding. Ever drive one?"

"I'm driving a friend's Jeep Cherokee now."

"Oh, yeah? Bought it here?"

"No, in the city."

"So, you were thinking of a Grand?" he asks, and nods

his head toward the big black one that stands inside the showroom.

"Now that I see it it might be a little too much car for me."

"Handles like a baby," he says. "You want to try it?"

"Why not?" I want to get him away from here.

"Let me get my jacket," Howard says.

We both stand up and I wander across the showroom.

Vreeland stops me with a question. He speaks so softly it's almost a whisper. "So why do you live there?"

"In the city? I like the beat."

"The beat? What's that mean?"

"Hard to explain."

Howard, wearing a green parka, says, "Ready?"

I nod and we go toward the door. In the background I hear Vreeland say, "The beat."

We go outside to a Grand Laredo that is identical to the one inside except it's green. The thing is so big it scares me but I dutifully climb into the driver's seat. Once there it doesn't feel that different from my Jeep. Howard hands me the key. And, while he does some cursory explaining about the vehicle, I give him the once-over.

There is no way to tell if someone is a killer by the way he looks. But you can size up a possible perp in other ways, like learning about social skills, moods, intelligence, living arrangements, to name a few. For instance, Howard has charm. He would have to to be a car salesman. But I watch and listen as he tries his charisma with me. I can see how it would work on others.

I start the Laredo and pull out onto the main road. It does handle wonderfully and is a smoother ride than our Jeep. I feel confident enough driving that I can engage Howard in conversation.

"Are you from around here, Mr. Howard?"

"Call me Lee. Yep, born here, always lived here."

"In Hallockville?"

"No, my parents still live here but I have my own place in Millquogue."

So he lives alone. Or does he? "Are you married?"

"No. I'm not sure I'll ever marry."

"Why's that?"

"Do you have children?" he asks.

"No."

"Well, I know this may sound odd, but I don't want children and most women do."

"It doesn't sound odd. Not everyone is meant to have children."

From the corner of my eye I can see he's smiling.

"It's a pleasure to meet someone who understands. Most people think I'm weird for not wanting kids."

"You have a girlfriend?"

"Oh, sure. We've only been dating for three months, don't live together. Kristin's something else though."

"How so?"

"Very independent. We ever marry I'm sure she'll keep Baxter, her last name."

I file away this information. "So she doesn't want children?"

"Tell you the truth, I haven't asked her. I don't want to spoil it."

"Smart," I say.

"Maybe I'll never bring it up."

"Would you like to live with her? Have you *ever* lived with a girlfriend?"

"Well, yes to both."

His tone tells me he's becoming suspicious about my questions. "Sorry to be so nosy, Lee, but I'm always interested in people, how they live, what they like to do." I glance his way, smile innocently.

"I understand. Me too."

I wait for him to tell me more, know he will.

"About four years ago I lived with my fiancée. But then . . . she was . . . murdered."

"Murdered?" I say with appropriate alarm.

"You ever hear of a son-of-a-bitch they call the Silk Scarf killer?"

"Yes. She was one of his victims?"

"Yeah. The second one. That's when we knew we had a serial killer on our hands."

It doesn't go by me that he's said *we* and *our*. This could refer to the population here but for some reason I don't think so. "We?"

"Well, the police. I'm sort of a buff."

My heart does a line dance! Police buffs are sometimes criminals. Not necessarily but it can be part of the profile. "You mean you hang out with the police?"

"Hey, I've known some of them my whole life. Guys I grew up and went to school with. Got a police scanner at home, too," he says proudly.

"So then you've been in on the investigation of the Silk Scarf murders?"

"Right. I'll tell you a secret but you've got to swear you won't say anything to anyone."

I pull the Laredo over to the side of the road and stop. I want to see him. "I promise," I say, looking into those startling blue eyes.

"There's been another one. Another murder. Today." He almost sounds giddy, like a small boy at show-and-tell.

"Happened on Sixth Street in Seaview," he continues. "Not official yet, but my friends told me about it."

"How awful," I say.

He rids himself of any expression that might look delighted and replaces it quickly with a mask of sorrow.

"Yeah. Terrible."

"Did you know her?"

"The victim? Not well. Judy Kempler. Thing is you sort of know everybody when you live in a small town. And the Kemplers lost a kid recently."

"Lost?"

He smiles in an almost seductive way. "Funny, isn't it, all the euphemisms people use for death? It was a hit-and-run. Now this. The husband, Sonny, will be devastated, to say the least."

"Who wouldn't be?"

"Yeah, yeah, of course."

I want to get back to him. "You must've been pretty upset yourself when your fiancée was murdered."

"Better believe it. Devastation doesn't cover it."

"Connie didn't want kids?"

He cocks his handsome head. "Yeah. How do you know?"

"Because you were going to marry her."

His eyes brighten with understanding. "Oh, I see, right. Yeah. She was unusual."

There's no way to let him know that I know Connie was trying to break up with him. If I do I'll give myself away. I touch his sleeve. "Sorry for your loss, Lee."

He turns, looks directly into my eyes. "Thanks, Lauren." There's not a shred of sincerity in those blue peepers and his voice rings hollow. Lee Howard is one scary guy.

Twelve

"So you'll think about it, right?" Lee said.

"I certainly will," Lauren said.

"It's a beaut. You can't go wrong with the Grand. And by the way, you drive like an angel."

When she smiled he knew he had her but he could hardly wait until she left. He stuck out his hand and when she took it he felt a slight wave of nausea.

"I'll get back to you," Lauren said.

Lee watched her go, kept standing outside until she was in her car and started up. Then he waved as she pulled out. He went back inside and told Vreeland he was going to the bank.

He got in his brown Dodge and pulled out of the lot, turned left on 25. At Parker Avenue he made a right and went up to the North Road, made a left, and pulled into the deli parking lot. He liked coming here at this hour because people left you alone, mostly because there were few people.

He was still shaking when he poured himself a container of coffee, which he took to a back table.

So who the hell was she? She sure as shit wasn't looking to buy a car. She'd said *Connie*. He thought he'd covered his shock when she said it but he couldn't be sure. How did she know her name was Connie? Well, how wasn't as important as the fact she knew it and knew something about him. In fact, was there to see him. Came especially to see him. But why?

Lee took a sip of the coffee. Good as always. Why the

hell had he brought up the murder of Judy Kempler? All it did was make him look bad if somebody was trying to find stuff on him. It had to have something to do with that goddamn Edith. She'd always believed he'd killed Connie. Never bought the serial-killer thing.

So what could it have to do with Edith? All those questions that woman was asking, about who he lived with and was he going to get married. What was wrong with him? Why hadn't he picked up on it? And what if she went scratching around looking for Kristin Baxter? Was Laurano some kind of private detective or something? Did Edith hire her?

Edith didn't have that kind of money. Those private dicks were expensive. But this one was a woman, maybe they came cheaper. And she hardly looked threatening. He could squash her with one hand if necessary. He had to find out who the hell she was.

Then he remembered who she said sent her. Volinewski. Would he know anything? If this Laurano *was* a private dick why would Volinewski hire her? What did he have to do with anything about him and Connie? Something was screwy, but maybe Volinewski could explain it.

Lee finished his coffee, waved to Dee behind the counter, and went out to his car. In his glove compartment was his duplicate phone book for this kind of an occasion. He rifled through it, found Volinewski's work number. He punched it into his car phone.

A woman answered saying it was Spring Realty and he asked for Stash. In a moment he came on the line. Lee made a little small talk and then did what he'd normally do.

"I wanted to thank you for sending Lauren Laurano to me."

"I didn't send her to you, Lee."

"You don't know the girl?"

"Yeah, sure. I rented a house to her but I don't recall mentioning you. I don't think we ever talked about cars. She looking to buy a car?"

"Said she was. Said you sent her."

"Nope. I rented her and three others a house on Spring Lane."

"Which house is that, Stash?"

"That big white one, sort of new. Across the street from the water. So she said I sent her, huh?"

"That's what she said."

"Maybe she used my name because I'm the only . . ." He trailed off.

Lee waited, had a feeling he was going to learn more. But then Volinewski didn't say anything. "What? What were you going to say?"

"Nothing. Just that she might have used my name because she doesn't know anyone else around here."

"Could be. What's she doing here, anyway?"

"Ah, working on another house in Seaview. Some friends bought a house there and the four of them are redoing it. Listen, Lee, I have another call. I'll talk to you soon, okay?"

And he was gone. Lee switched off the phone. Volinewski knew something he didn't want to tell him. Lee started his car and drove out of the parking lot onto the North Road, headed toward Benny's Beach.

There was no question in his mind that Laurano was after something, after him, maybe. But why? And who was behind it? He was pretty sure his cop friends wouldn't know but he'd put out a feeler when he could. Right now they were all involved in the Kempler murder.

When he hit the water at Benny's Beach he turned left on Spring. He was pretty sure he knew which house Volinewski meant but he wanted to be sure. Yeah, there it was, right in the middle of the block. Good. Worse came to worst he knew where to find her.

Thirteen

It's time to call it a day. I head toward Seaview. The sky is growing dark with wintry weather and the shortening days. I'm not too happy about my progress so far. Of course, I let myself get sidetracked by the Silk Scarf serial killer. But what detective wouldn't? Whether Howard is a copycat killer is a whole other question. Maybe Kuerstiner's death is yet another unsolved crime having nothing to do with anything else.

Still, I have to remember what I've been hired to do: unearth the person who murdered Bill Moffat, or find that it was a suicide.

I turn into the Js' street and can't see if the car's still there until I cross the railroad tracks. It's there. Part of me sighs because I don't want to get roped into painting or anything else. The truth is I hate doing work like this. I only agreed to it because we're such good friends and they've been there for us.

I pull in the driveway. When I get out of the car a man approaches me from next door.

"Good evening," he says.

He's tall and hunched over like the bend in a tree branch. He wears a blue watch cap, pea jacket, and jeans. Because of the quickly fading light it's hard to see his features clearly, but I note that they're large, leaning toward gross.

"I'm your next-door neighbor," he says, holding out a huge hand.

"No, I'm not here," I answer stupidly. "I mean, this isn't my house."

"Oh." He drops his hand against his side. "I thought that two women bought the place."

"They did. But I'm not one of them. They're inside. I'm a friend."

"I see. Well, I'm still the next-door neighbor," he says and laughs lightly. "My name's Eugene Bennett. Most people call me Bennett."

"Hi, I'm Lauren Laurano."

Bennett brings up his hand and I take it. "Very alliterative," he says.

I smile, unable to say anything, as I've heard this many times.

"They going to put up a fence or anything?"

"I don't know. Would you like to meet them?"

"Well, yes, I would."

I wonder what I've done but it's too late. I lead Bennett into the house. "Hi," I yell. "Brought someone with me."

Total silence. But right away I notice the amazing change inside. Everything I can see is white, even though it's clearly a first coat.

"Hello? Anybody here?"

First Kip then the Js step into view from the back of the house, stare at me and my guest.

"This is Eugene Bennett, your next-door neighbor."

"Everyone calls me Bennett," he says.

The Js put down their paintbrushes and come toward us. They introduce themselves to Bennett and there's some desultory conversation. Right before he's ready to leave, Bennett says:

"You planning to put up a fence or anything?"

"We haven't thought about it," says Jenny.

I know this to be untrue because it was one of the first things she said she was going to do.

"I like that you took down that stupid structure, but a fence, unless it's real low, wouldn't look good."

Jill says, "We have a dog so we'll have to do something."

"Yeah, I guess. As long as it's the kind you don't see. . . . You know, like chicken wire covered by the bushes."

The mention of chicken wire gets a grimace from Jenny.

"So, it's nice to meet you. You need any help with anything, any advice as to where to buy stuff, you let me or my wife, Marge, know."

They thank him and accompany him to the door. When they come back in I raise both hands in surrender. "I didn't know what to do. I'm sorry."

"Had to happen sooner or later," Jenny says. "What a dork."

Kip comes from the back. "You *are* putting up a fence, aren't you?"

"As soon as I can," Jenny answers. "Stockade. Six feet."

After dinner, which I have to make because they don't consider what I've done with my day work, everyone goes to bed early.

Kip lies on the floor of our bedroom doing back exercises while Nick and Nora watch, and I finish telling her about my day.

"So now you're going to chase a serial killer, too? I don't believe this."

"I didn't say that."

"You don't have to *say* it, Lauren."

"I stumbled across this. I didn't go out looking for it. Don't you think it's interesting that there's a serial killer on this small piece of Long Island?"

"Interesting isn't the word I'd choose."

She's being difficult and I don't know what it is I'm supposed to say. Promise that I won't get involved. I can't do that. "You want me to give up my life, don't you?"

"What could that possibly mean?" Kip sits up.

"It means what it says. You don't want me to do this work anymore, do you?"

"That isn't true. What do you base that on?"

"Your whole attitude."

"*My* attitude?"

"Don't start, Kip."

She looks at me innocently with those beagle brown eyes. "I haven't the vaguest idea of what you're talking about."

I know this is a lie. "Let's face it, ever since . . . the incident . . . you've been holding me hostage."

Standing up, she says, "The incident? Hostage? You've got to be kidding. Since when is having an affair an *incident?*"

"Okay. . . ever since the affair you've been making me pay, in one form or another."

"Lauren, that simply isn't true." She picks up Nick and sits on the end of the bed with him. He lies on his back in her arms, like a baby. "How have I made you pay? Name the ways."

I hate it when she does this. "You know I won't be able to think of a single thing."

"I don't know. You said I've made you pay ever since the affair and I want to know how."

"Little things."

"Like what?"

Nick opens his mouth in his soundless cry and it's exactly how I feel.

"I don't know, I can't think right now. What do you want from me, anyway?"

She puts her hand on my arm. "Reassure me," she says, softly.

"About what?

"Alex, of course."

"I don't know what more I can say, Kip. I'm not in love with her, I never was, I never wanted to leave you for her, and I haven't seen her since that awful day."

"And you don't want to?" she prompts.

"And I don't want to."

"And you never think about her?"

Oh, boy. "I can't tell you that. I do think about her but not the way you probably mean. I sometimes wonder how she's doing. She's not in a great relationship and I worry that she's settling for something she shouldn't."

"Do you feel you're settling?"

"Of course not. Oh, Kip." I reach for her and Nick jumps down. I take her in my arms but she seems reluctant, stiff.

"Sometimes," she says, "it feels like we'll never work this out. Never get beyond all this."

"You mean Alex?"

"Alex. The money thing."

"Kip, as far as I'm concerned we're already beyond the Alex thing. I am, anyway. And you could be if you'd forgive me."

She abruptly pulls out of my arms and jumps up. "Oh, Christ, you're a brat. Do you hear what you've said? You've put the ball in my court, made me the villain. *I* have to forgive *you* for us to be okay."

"That's not how I meant it."

"Really? What else could that mean?"

"I meant that if you could let it go, the Alex affair, believe that I'm sorry, I think it would help us both."

"Do you regret your affair with her?"

I've been waiting for this question, knowing someday it would come, and I'm distressed that it's finally happened. I know this could be a deal breaker but I have to be honest. "No."

She looks as though I've slapped her.

"Kip, please try to understand. I regret hurting you but not having the affair. I believe that having the affair with Alex saved our marriage. I don't know where we'd be now if I hadn't. It's made us look at our relationship and try to fix the things that eventually would've killed it."

"So now you're saying you *saved* our relationship? You're incredible, Lauren."

"You don't want to talk about this, you want to punish me."

"Where's that coming from?"

"You won't hear what I'm saying."

"What I hear is you saying you saved our relationship by sleeping with that child."

"Stop."

"Well, that's what you said."

"Listen to me, Kip. You asked me if I regret it and I'm saying I don't because it forced some issues. I think we were in a pit and something had to give. I don't advocate that everyone should have an affair when their relationship is in trouble, but I am saying that in our case it happened to work that way. I also think our marriage is strong enough to withstand it, to go beyond it. Isn't it?"

"I don't know."

This stings but I press on. "I think the question is, has been, is this marriage worth saving?"

We look at each other for a long time; neither says anything. Then she says, "I do, you know."

"Do what?"

"Forgive you."

"Since when?"

"Since now."

I laugh. "Thank you. So then I guess you think it is worth saving."

"Yes. Don't you?"

"Do you love me?" I ask, timorously.

"Yes. Very much."

We come together and our lips meet in a long meaningful kiss filled with the years of all the things that go into any marriage, both good and bad.

When we part she says, "I think we can work it out."

"I know we can," I say. And that's the truth.

Fourteen

At breakfast Jill says, "You working on your case today, Lauren?"

"Yep. There are several people I have to see, interview."

"Such as?" Jenny asks.

"Police, for one. And I want to talk to Moffat's wife."

"Shouldn't the funeral be today?" asks Kip.

"Tomorrow. They did an autopsy. I want to see that report. I wonder how cooperative the Seaview Police will be."

"You're going to see the dead guy's wife today?" Jill asks, sounding dismayed.

Although I've shared some of my cases with the Js they've never been close to one on a daily basis.

"I have to see everybody who's connected."

"It seems so, I don't know, callous or something," Jill says.

A splash of guilt washes over me but is gone in an instant as I know this is a necessary component of my job.

"I can understand why you see it that way, Jill, but it goes with the territory."

"Yeah, but the guy's not even in the ground yet and you have to meet with his wife? If anything happened to Jenny I wouldn't be able to talk to a detective, or anybody, for weeks."

"Weeks?" Jenny says. "What about months?"

"Years," says Jill.

"Look," I say, "I know it sounds heartless and all, but I can't think about it that way."

They are all looking at me as though I'm Dr. Frankenstein. "What?"

"I'm glad I don't have your job," Jill says.

Now they're starting to piss me off.

"It's a dirty job but somebody has to do it," Kip says, and I know this is her way of showing she's behind me, giving me support.

I smile at her.

We gather up our breakfast dishes, dump them into the dishwasher, put on our winter clothes so we all look like Charlie Brown, and make our way to our respective cars. I kiss Kip good-bye and tell them I'll drop in later.

I notice that I'm low on gas so I pull into the first station I see. I don't know how to pump my own so I go to the full-serve area. Well, it's not that I don't know how, it's that I hate it. I never wanted to be a gas station attendant. Why should I start now? I power down my window and turn off the motor.

As I rummage in my purse for my wallet I feel a person hovering. I turn to look and find a woman standing there. This in itself wouldn't be unusual, or anything to marvel at, but this *particular* woman is another story.

"Help ya?" she asks.

"Fill it with regular," I manage to eke out between shocked lips.

"Sure thing."

I try not to let her see I'm staring as I turn to watch her. She's tall and skinny and has a head of curls the color of a Dole pineapple. The makeup job is almost revolutionary. Glitter covers her cheeks like freckles and what's around her eyes brings the word *raccoon* to mind. But the most astonishing thing is what she wears on her feet. Black pumps with three-inch heels each the width of a pencil. The rest of her attire is skin-tight black jeans and a short brown leather jacket.

When she finishes and tucks away the pump she comes

back to tell me what I owe. I try, I swear I try, but can't help myself, and I almost cry when I hear the words of my mother come from my mouth: "Aren't you cold in that short jacket?" Oh, God.

"Nah, I'm always movin' around."

I nod stupidly, manage to refrain from being a worse geezer with further inane questions, ask what I owe, pay, and get the hell out of there.

The Seaview Police, it seems, have new headquarters near the train station, facing the harbor. I park and take the boardwalk that leads to the door.

Inside it looks nothing like any police station I've ever frequented. In N.Y.C. the walls are painted green, or in need of paint, and there's always a feeling of death, a smell of insecticide.

This place is cream-cheese white and the front desk is made of white filing cabinets with a black top across them. It's almost a designer look. The cop behind the desk is young, his brown hair short, a face like a surfacing porpoise. The name on the desk is Sgt. Bert Lockwood.

He looks up, gives me a surreptitious once-over but I catch it anyway.

"Kin I help you?"

I give him my small starry smile. "I hope so."

He bites, smiles back. "What's the problem?"

"Well, Sergeant Lockwood, it's not exactly a problem. I'm a private investigator and —"

"— A what?"

Oh, boy. I show him my license.

"Whaddaya know. So what's up?"

"I was wondering if you could tell me about the autopsy report on Bill Moffat?"

"Yer kidding."

"No."

"I can't do that. I mean, yer not official."

"Does that matter?"

He does a pantomime of thinking, which includes the

cliché of scratching his head. "I'm not supposed to give out that information to just anybody."

"Well, maybe I could talk to the chief."

He glances toward a closed door, back to me. "Chief Wagner's pretty busy."

"Could you ask?" I say, still pleasant.

After a beat, he slides back his black desk chair, gets up, goes to the door, knocks once, disappears inside. He returns in a moment.

Sounding surprised, he says, "He'll see ya."

"Thanks."

He opens the door for me. "Chief, this is . . . ah . . ."

"Lauren Laurano."

"Yeah, Laurano."

The chief motions me in as Lockwood closes the door behind me. Wagner is a big man, his upper body high above the desktop. He has dyed black hair or a toupee, I can't tell which, and pale skin like frost. His eyes are brown and too small for his face, which has a prominent nose and thin lips.

"Sit down," he says.

I do. This room is even less like the stations I'm used to. I sit in a blue armchair, and a matching couch is against one wall.

"So what can I do for you?"

Oh, boy. I ask him about Moffat.

He runs a chunky hand over his mouth and chin, the way men do. "Well, we're not used to giving out such to people we don't know."

"I can appreciate that, sir, but surely it'll be public soon."

"But not yet," he says, as though he's one-upped me.

"Is there a problem with it?" I say, trying to put the onus on him.

"Problem?" He clears his throat, shifts in his chair. "No problem. There's nothing to hide, after all. Straight suicide."

"Nothing that indicates Moffat could've been hanged, murdered?"

Wagner laughs, a sound like dozens of eggs cracking.

"Murdered? Never heard of a murder like that, hanging a person."

"Always a first time," I say, perhaps too jauntily.

He eyes me peculiarly. "Where'd you get such a notion?"

"It wasn't my idea."

"You been hired by some ditz, right?"

"I've been hired, yes."

"Has to be a ditz to think it was murder. Must've been his whore."

I flinch at his word, thinking of Alison, who's anything but. "I can't tell you who hired me."

"Doesn't matter. You're wasting your time, you know. Well, no, I guess not. You're being paid. So your client's wasting her money, but then that's her problem, isn't it?" He smiles, lips like lean bird legs.

"What makes you think it's a woman?"

"No man would hire you. Don't mean *you* personally, but no man around here would hire a lady dick. So it's gotta be the whore or his wife."

"Why do you keep calling Ms. Von Elder a whore?"

"What *should* I call a female who sleeps with another woman's man?"

"Are you friends with Mrs. Moffat?"

"Friends? Not strictly. I know Toby all her life, but not intimate, you know what I mean."

"It must've been awful when their child died."

Wagner's eyes flash uneasiness. "Terrible thing." He looks away from me, stares at a fancy wall calendar displaying a Picasso.

The certain feeling that I've hit on something overtakes me. I press on. "What exactly happened to him?"

"Him?"

"Yes. Freddy."

"Freddy was a girl. Frederica."

I don't know why I'm so taken aback, but I am. I suppose it was because I'd been picturing a little boy in my mind. Still.

"What happened to her?"

"Accident. Now, Mrs. Laurano, what else can I do for you?"

Chief Wagner absolutely doesn't want to talk about the death of Freddy Moffat. Why?

"You can tell me what kind of accident."

"What's this got to do with anything?" he asks, gruffly.

"Is there some reason you don't want to talk about it?"

"Why would there be a reason? The thing is, I'm a busy man."

They are always *busy men*, as though this makes any difference.

"It's a simple question," I say, acting bewildered.

"I don't see where this is leading or what it's to do with Moffat's suicide."

"I'd like to know," I say firmly.

The chief presses those slit lips together so they disappear, then tells me. "Took a fall. Wandered away from her yard. Missing a few days until we found her bottom of one of the Sound bluffs. Tragic."

I almost say, *Now was that so hard?*, but bite my tongue. Still, I wonder why it *was* so hard.

"Anything else?" he barks, ostentatiously looking at his watch.

Funny how his attitude toward me has changed since I brought up Freddy. I rise. "No, you've been very helpful. There is one more thing."

He sighs.

"The serial killer you have here."

This produces a cheek tic. "What about him?"

"Any leads?"

"Not at liberty to tell you that. A word of advice, Laurano."

The lack of the *Mrs.* is not lost on me.

"You have to ply your trade here, stick to what you been hired to do. That's pushing it, as it is."

"I hear you," I say pleasantly.

We shake hands and I notice his is cold although the room isn't.

Back in my car I sit, wondering. There's something about

Freddy Moffat's death that sticks in the chief's craw. And he doesn't want me messing around with the serial-killer case either. Of course, all cops, except Cecchi and maybe Michelle Lent, are like this. They don't want P.I.s, whom they regard with contempt, anywhere near their cases. Still, the chief's reaction seemed like more than the usual disdain. I file my reaction, start the Jeep, and head out toward Toby Moffat's house.

Fifteen

Chief Wagner stared at the door after Laurano left and thought, *What the hell is this now?* If it isn't one damn thing it's another. Didn't he have enough on his plate? Now he had to worry about some stupid girl detective. He twirled his Rolodex and found the number he wanted, then punched it in.

"Toby?" he said when she answered. "Chief Wagner, sorry to bother you."

"That's all right, Chief."

"How you doing?"

"As well as can be expected."

"Right. Naturally. I guess I haven't told you I'm sorry for your loss."

"Thanks."

"Thing is, Toby, reason I'm calling is, I was wondering if you lost faith in us or what?"

"I don't understand."

He smoothed his toupee, smiled. "The girl you hired, the detective."

She was silent for a moment and he thought maybe Toby was the one. Then she said, "Girl? Detective?"

"Let's see. Laurano, her name is. She told me you hired her, thinking maybe Bill was murdered."

Toby gasped slightly. "No. I never heard of her."

"Thought she might be giving me a load of bull. Now, Toby, you don't think that, do you? That Bill was murdered?"

This time the silence went on.

"Toby?" Wagner leaned forward, both elbows on his desk.

"Yes, I'm here."

"Well, do you?"

"It's hard for me to accept Billy committed suicide," she said softly.

So she did think he was murdered. There was going to be trouble about this. Besides, if Toby didn't hire this girl, then who did? "Toby, every indication shows it was suicide. I know you don't want to believe that of Bill but there's no other explanation."

"I don't know what to say, Chief."

"You like me to come see you?" This was the last thing he needed to do now.

"No, that's okay. Thanks."

"Well, you need anything give me a call, will you?"

"Yes. Thanks."

He got off with a few more encouraging words and then stared stupidly at the phone. So, it had to be the whore who hired the girl. Should he pay her a call? He didn't know her and what the hell could he say? Fact was, she had a right to hire anyone she damn pleased.

He didn't like the questions about Freddy's death either. He didn't even like to think about that. One thing could lead to another.

Ah, hell. If his department and the county police couldn't figure things out, what was this bitch detective going to come up with anyways? Still, it made him uneasy. He'd better have a meeting with the boys . . . sooner the better.

Sixteen

Unassuming is the best adjective I can think of for the Moffat place. It's a shingled farmhouse set in the midst of fields, although it isn't isolated since other houses are visible from it.

I park in the driveway, walk up the path. Parti-colored dried corn hangs on the door. I don't see a bell or knocker so I use my knuckles to rap my arrival. She's expecting me; I called ahead.

But when she opens the door I'm not expecting the person I see. Toby Moffat is beautiful; grief-stricken, but beautiful. She's of medium height and has a small frame. Dark hair with real red highlights touches her shoulders. She has almond-shaped eyes, a straight narrow nose, and full lips. The only makeup I detect is a faint blush of lipstick. A white overshirt, with a purple turtleneck beneath, is worn over black leggings.

"Lauren Laurano?"

"Yes."

"Please come in."

The house has a sprawling feel to it. The living room is large and airy and there are several couches with colorful slipcovers and well-worn easy chairs. A large round coffee table is littered with magazines, and there are floor-to-ceiling bookcases on three of the four walls. The hardwood floor is covered by a dispirited rug. Toby sits on one of the couches and I take an armchair. She offers me something to drink and I decline.

"Thank you for seeing me, Mrs. Moffat."

She tells me to call her Toby. "I welcome your interest. The police certainly won't help. As a matter of fact, Chief Wagner called me before you did and asked if I'd hired you."

I ponder this statement but don't press it.

"Of course I told him no. I don't know who hired you and I don't care. The police will never pursue this case. The same way they ignored my child's death."

At the mention of this her face collapses like an abandoned hand puppet.

I try to be as gentle as possible. "I thought your daughter's death was an accident."

The eyes flare with anger. "That's what they wanted us to believe, what they wanted everyone to believe."

They. My heart always falters when *they* are invoked. It's so often the pronoun of paranoids or conspiracy devotees. As delicately as possible, I ask who *they* are.

Toby smiles, twisted like a river. "You think I'm nuts, don't you?"

Apparently I'm not as skillful as I'd thought. "Not at all." This is true; my assessment of her isn't that harsh.

She laughs bitterly. "I've been through all this before."

"Through what?"

"The nonbelievers, the scorn."

I'm bewildered that she agreed to meet with me if she supposes this. "Please don't think that about me, Toby. I have no preconceived ideas."

"No one's talked to you about me?"

"Not in the way you mean, no. I'm interested in what you have to say."

She stares at me as though she'll be able to determine the validity of this. Finally, she says, "Freddy was murdered, like Bill was."

I'm startled by her words and yet I believe them. I don't know why. "Tell me more," I say.

She brightens, sensing my faith in her. "I wish I could tell you with certainty who's responsible, but I can't. Still want me to go on?"

I nod.

"I believe Freddy was abducted and then murdered. No one called for ransom or anything like that, but I know she wouldn't have wandered off."

"If there was no ransom demand why do you think she was taken?"

"I don't know who took her, but I know it happened," she says, evading my question. "When she was found at the bottom of that bluff the police did nothing. I begged. But they ignored me. Chief Wagner said I was a 'distraught mother.' Well, that was true. I was. Probably still am. But that wasn't why I thought what I did. Freddy wasn't the first kid from these parts to disappear and later be found dead due to an accident. She was the second."

"Really?"

"Yes, really," she snaps.

"I didn't mean —"

"Sorry. I'm so used to skepticism."

"Can we get this settled, Toby? I'm here because I want to help. It's true that I've been hired to look into your husband's death but it may all be connected."

"Oh, it is," she says with conviction.

My detective's heart droops as I detect a conspiracy theory. I move to something else. "Who was the other child who had an accident?"

"Other two. There was a third. One after Freddy. I'll write their names down for you. One was from Southedges and one from Seaview. Both girls. The first one, Mary Lavin, the one from the South Fork, was gone for about three days, no ransom asked for, and then found in what appeared to be an accident. I believed it until it happened to Freddy. The third one was killed by a hit-and-run but she hadn't disappeared beforehand. Still, I believe the same thing might have happened to her."

"Why?"

"Because now her mother's dead."

Something dawns on me. "Wait a minute . . . are you talking about the Kemplers?"

"Yes. Exactly. The child, Bebe, was a hit-and-run victim, and now Judy's been murdered. Don't you think that's odd?"

"I do."

"Billy was getting close to an answer. He wouldn't tell me what it was, said he didn't want me in danger, but I have my own ideas. I think the killer of these children is the Silk Scarf murderer."

"Why?"

"Because it's too much. Too much in such a small area. A place that's usually peaceful and has a low crime rate. How could there be two killers on the loose?"

This wasn't a crazy assumption, if you accepted that the three children were actually murdered. I don't know what I believe at this point.

"What about Bill?"

"Bill was murdered too. He never would've hung himself. Not now. When Freddy died, maybe then. No. Not even then. That's not who he was."

"So you think Bill was murdered because he'd uncovered some truths?"

"Absolutely."

I try to temper the next question with complete conviction. "Toby, you said *they* were covering up. Who did you mean?"

"The police. The officials. That much Bill hinted at. He said I'd never believe who was involved, that it was going to rock the people here to their toes."

"When you say officials . . . who's that?"

"Well, I'm not sure. Local government, I guess."

"I don't know anything about how you're governed here."

"Seaview is the only town with a mayor. The rest of the township, including Seaview, has a supervisor. And there's a town board."

"And you think these are the people Bill was referring to?"

"Look, don't think I don't know how wild this sounds, but there's no one else he could've meant."

"What's the name of the supervisor?"

"Julian Perini. He's been supervisor so long I can't even remember who it was he originally beat. They're corrupt, Lauren. All of them."

"Chief Wagner as well?"

"Absolutely. In lots of ways. But I don't care about the skimming and turning a blind eye to the drug dealing. Well, I do care, but my real concern is the deaths of my daughter and husband."

"Of course. What about FEAG?"

"What about them?"

"Your husband opposed them, didn't he?"

"Yes. Sure. Any sane person would. Wait a minute, you think the FEAG people had something to do with Bill's murder?"

"It's been suggested."

She slowly shakes her head. "No. I can't buy that. They're unscrupulous, but killing someone to get their way? And what good would it do to get rid of Bill? That's not going to stop fast food coming here."

"Couldn't it serve as a warning to the AFF people?"

"Has it?"

"I don't know," I say, honestly. "I can only say that some are frightened."

"I see," she says, as though now she understands the nature of the universe.

"You loved your husband, didn't you?"

"Yes. Don't you love yours?" Her eyes focus on my wedding ring.

"I don't have a husband, but I love my partner, yes."

"Partner. A man or a woman?"

"Woman." I feel the slight thump in my chest I always do when I reveal my lesbianism to a heterosexual whom I don't know, having no idea what the reaction will be.

"Been together long?"

"Sixteen years."

"Bill and I were together eighteen," she says wistfully.
What about Alison? I wonder.

As though reading my mind she says, "You're thinking, Bill had a mistress, so what is she talking about, aren't you?"

"Something like that."

"You'll probably think I'm a fool but that never came between us. I'm not a jealous woman, never have been. He needed her for some reason and it made our relationship better. Now you're thinking I was some sort of patsy, in denial, told myself this to keep my man. Right?"

"I don't know what to think. If what you say is true, you have to admit, it's pretty unusual."

"I didn't say it wasn't."

"This is none of my business but . . ."

"Oh, you mean, the rest *was* your business?" She grins.

I like her. "Got me."

"Ask away."

"I heard you were a drinker. You don't look like any drinker I've ever known."

"I've been sober for five months."

"Ah. And your drinking had nothing to do with Bill and his . . . his girlfriend?"

"I think it had to do with the fact that I'm an alcoholic and Freddy's death was an excuse to drink more."

I know alcoholism is a disease so I don't question what she means. But I'm still bewildered by her attitude about Alison. Am I thinking of Alex, wishing Kip felt the same way?

"You were *never* jealous of Alison?"

"I had moments in the beginning but he convinced me he loved me and, let's face it, he didn't leave me."

"You're an amazing woman, Toby."

"You're right." She laughs.

I have to ask the question she didn't answer earlier. "Why do you think the children were abducted and killed?"

A haunted expression plays across her face. "Well, it didn't show up on the autopsy, and I can't explain that, but I think these children were sexually abused."

"By the Silk Scarf killer?"

"Why not?"

"I have to tell you it would be unusual for a man, and I assume the killer's a man, to be interested in both children and grown women."

"Is it possible?"

"Anything's possible."

"But you don't think so."

"It would be unusual," I repeat. "And if sexual abuse didn't show up on Freddy's autopsy report . . ." I shrug.

"Maybe there is more than one killer?" she says, sounding desperate.

"You made a good case for one, but I have an easier time believing there are two. Still, why would the police, the officials, cover up all this?"

"I don't know. Unless one of the killers is a prominent person, or there are lots of people involved."

"A child pornography ring?"

"Yes," she says eagerly. "Yes. That makes sense. If it could happen in Belgium why couldn't it happen here?"

She has a point.

I rise. "Would you write down the names of everyone you think is involved?"

"You bet I will."

In my car I look over the list. If Toby's right and local officials are involved somehow, this could be a tricky and dangerous business for me. Maybe I should get Cecchi's advice. Nothing like having input from a New York City cop. Even an ex one.

For a long time I resisted having a cellular phone. I used to run all over New York City looking for a phone booth, only to be confronted with broken, smelly, or occupied ones. But I didn't want to look like all those people on the streets walking around with phones. Finally I had to give in and get myself one. I have to admit, it's handy. And then Kip got a car phone, which is also handy.

I pull over to the side of the road because I don't like to

drive and talk. I punch in Cecchi's number. He never went back to the department after he was shot because he couldn't face a desk job. So he's at home and when I get back, we're going into business together. But there's no reason we can't start now. He answers after one ring, which tells me how bored he is.

After some idle chitchat I fill him in.

"You're going to go after a whole town by yourself?" he asks incredulously.

"I thought I might. But then I thought I better check it out with you and that's what I'm doing so don't give me a headache." Static prickles my ear.

"Listen, Lauren, I'm counting on you to get my life back on track. I thought we were going to be partners."

"We are." God, he's gotten so self-involved since the shooting. Cecchi is married to Annette, a classy dame, as an old friend of mine would've said. He's an unusual man and was an unusual cop. He doesn't know what to do with himself anymore. I have an idea.

"Why don't you come out here and help me?"

"What are you, crazy?"

"What's so crazy about it?"

"Me in the sticks?"

"I know, I know. But it isn't the sticks. I mean, they have bagels and movies and a helluva lot of crime."

"Yeah? Bagels? How good could they be?"

"Pretty good. Not H&H, but okay. I wouldn't lie about a thing like a bagel. Look, it's Thursday. Tomorrow night come with Annette. We have an extra room in this big house."

"What about the others? They wouldn't mind?"

"Of course not. They all love you and Annette."

"Lemme think about it."

"Until when?"

"At least let me talk to Annette when she comes home from work. What would she do out there?"

"Rest, relax."

"I don't know. She's not too good at that."

"Talk her into it. We'll work and we'll have some fun."

"You actually got a client? A paying one?"

"Sure." I know it's not enough for us both but he doesn't really care.

"Lemme think about it, talk to Annette."

"Okay. I'll call you later."

"Lauren? You watch your behind, okay?"

"Right."

When we hang up I go completely into my manipulative mode and dial Annette. I learned it at my mother's knee.

Seventeen

Annette has agreed to get Cecchi to come out here. I hope I haven't underestimated my housemates. I know Kip won't mind, and Jenny and Jill like Cecchi and Annette. But they might not feel like living with them, even if it's only for a few days. I guess I should've asked them first.

As I drive back to Seaview I notice a feeling of happiness brought on by the fulgent light that hits the water when I cross the causeway. Oh no. Am I being seduced by the country? It's not that I don't want Kip to be right . . . it's that I don't want Kip to be right.

Kip.

This hasn't been easy for her. It hasn't been easy for either of us but in different ways. I know it's affected her self-esteem, and as much as I know my affair with Alex didn't make me love Kip any less, I can understand why she'd have trouble believing that, or thinking of herself as desirable to me. It's been hard on me because I feel I have to prove my love all the time. And hard, let's face it, because I still think about Alex. Not that I want to be with her, but the excitement, the drama, that insanity isn't there anymore and I miss it. And when I hear love songs it's Alex I think of, not Kip. It all has to do with fantasy. . . . I know this, I do. Still, there's nothing quite like those early days with someone. I suppose that's why people move on to the next one all the time, especially those of us (read gays and lesbians) who can't get married legally. It's so easy. I don't want to go from person to person, yet it's hard to think I'll never have that feeling again. What I feel for Kip is much more profound, but it isn't titillating.

Love is a nightmare.

I pop into the drugstore and look in the phone book for Kristin Baxter, Lee Howard's girlfriend. She's listed. I punch in the numbers. A woman answers. I ask for Kristin and she tells me she's at work. I ask where work is and she becomes reticent.

"Seems to me if you were a friend of Kristin's you'd know where she works."

"I didn't say I was a friend." I explain who I am.

"A private detective?" she says, unbelieving.

"That's right. If you don't want to tell me where she works I understand. I'll find out another way."

"Is it about Lee Howard?"

My detective's heart races like the moon. But I'm not sure why. It would be natural for her to ask about Ms. Baxter's fiancé, wouldn't it? Why don't I believe this?

"It is," I say.

"Well, I guess it wouldn't hurt then. She works in the Seaview branch of the North Shore Bank."

I start to ask where that is but think I've gotten enough from this woman so I thank her and hang up. Behind the cosmetic counter is a woman who looks like she's wearing all the makeup they're selling.

"C'n I help you?" She has a high squeaky voice.

"Maybe."

"Bet I can." She blinks heavily laden lashes at me and if I didn't know better I'd think she was flirting. "We have a great new perfume on sale. Called Mystery."

Just what I need. "No, I don't want perfume, I —"

"How about this new lipstick, fab color. Called Heliotrope Heaven. Oh, you don't wear lipstick, do you?"

"No, I —"

"You should, you know. You need color. Pale is what you are."

"Thank you. Look, all I want is —"

"A base. You need a base. Is that what you want?"

"A base?"

"Yes. I think your color would be —"

"No, please. I want some directions, that's all."

She looks at me with pity.

"Well, honey, there's nothing hard about learning to make up your face. I don't think I have any printed directions but I can tell you."

I can't help smiling. "Directions to the North Shore Bank."

"Ahhh."

She gives them to me.

I walk because it's not far and I get a better sense of the town this way. It seems to me that a lot of stores are empty but I see a bookstore I hadn't noticed before. It's called Heartwell's and I can't control myself from stepping inside.

I'm immediately disappointed because there's nothing inviting or bookish about it. Maybe I could open a better one here. Am I crazy? What am I thinking? I get the hell out of there as fast as I can.

At the end of the street I turn left, pass a cheese and gourmet shop, and find myself at the bank. Inside, it's a bank. Surprise. I go to a teller and ask for Kristin Baxter. The teller points to a young woman sitting at a desk. I thank her and walk over to the woman.

She's working on something and when she looks up I see that she's quite beautiful, with jet black hair and eyes that match. Her makeup is minimal, light lipstick, some eye shadow. She wears a tan cashmere suit, white blouse. When she smiles she's a stunner.

"How can I help you?"

I produce my license and for a moment she looks concerned, and then I tell her I want to talk to her about Lee Howard.

She rolls her eyes heavenward and I get a rush of adrenaline.

"Finally," she says.

"Finally?"

"Somebody is doing something about that dork."

"Dork," I repeat. "Then he's not your fiancé?"

"Fiancé?" She laughs, a tinkle of wind chimes. "About three years ago I made the mistake of going out with him *once*. I was bored or something, I guess. And boy, have I lived to regret it."

"Why's that?"

"Have you ever met him?"

"I have."

"Well, doesn't he give you the creeps?" She shudders and runs her hands up and down her arms as though she were cold.

"Tell me about him. About what you mean."

"It's hard to explain. I went out on this date with him and nothing out of the ordinary happened. I mean, he took me to dinner and a movie and didn't even try to hit on me when he took me home. But I knew I never wanted to go out with him again."

"And you can't say why?"

"Well, you've seen him, you know he's handsome, so it's not that; but there's something about the way he looks at you. Anyway, what happened afterward, and has been happening ever since, confirmed everything I felt."

"What happened?"

"He called me for another date and I said no but he kept calling so I said I was seeing someone else, which, by the way, is the truth." She turns around a framed picture on her desk of a nice-looking young man. "Dan Ostrander."

"He's cute," I say.

"Yeah, he is." She looks at the picture longingly before she puts it back in its spot.

"Lee," I remind her.

"Right. Well, after that he stopped calling but he started stalking me. Every place I'd go I'd see him. And he followed me in his car."

"What'd you do about it?"

"The first thing I did was in a store. I went up to him and told him right out to stop. You know what he did? He smiled. Said, 'How are you, Kristin?' Oh, God, he's such a creep."

"And the next thing you did?"

"I went to the police. Didn't do a damn bit of good. He still kept stalking me but never when I was with Dan."

"Who'd you speak to at the police?"

"Bert Lockwood."

"And he said they'd talk to Howard?"

"He did. I don't think anyone ever talked to him."

I don't either.

"Ms. Baxter, Lee Howard told me you were his fiancée."

"Oh, Lord. He tells everyone that. Dan wanted to pay him a visit but I told him not to. I mean, I don't want them fighting or anything. It's all too weird."

"Why do you think he says that? That you're his fiancée?"

"I haven't the vaguest. But I wish he'd stop."

"Did you consider going back to the police?"

"For what? They aren't about to do anything. They're all 'old boys,' if you know what I mean?"

I nod. "Well, thank you for your time." I start to get up.

"Tell me, is he stalking someone else? I mean, how come you're on his case?"

"I can't go into that. But Howard's a side issue. I'm afraid no one's hired me to go after him."

"Maybe *I* should hire you."

"There's nothing I could do about him. But I'll be watching him while I'm on this other thing."

"Any help getting the creep out of my life would be appreciated."

"I'll do what I can."

We shake hands and I leave the bank, walk back toward my Jeep. So what should I make of this development? That Howard's a creep is no surprise. That he told me Baxter was his fiancée is. I guess he didn't think I'd check. But what's his need to say this? And is she really safe? I wonder if I should call him on this. No, I decide. I think it's better and safer to keep a low profile with Lee Howard.

Since I'm here I decide to interview the mayor of Seaview, who is also the owner of a bake shop, which is next to the theater. It's called Luke's Bakery. To the point, you'd have to say.

Eighteen

When I open the door a bell tinkles. The smell is delicious. I guess there's nothing more inviting than the aroma of baking bread, which is the overriding odor, although I can detect chocolate in the mix.

In the glass case are cakes and pies, tarts, brownies, and cookies. I avert my eyes and look at the face of the woman behind the counter.

Her brown hair is pulled back in a ponytail. An old green cardigan over a light blue turtleneck keeps her warm.

"I'd like to see Luke Latham, please."

"Can I say who wants to see him?"

At least she doesn't ask me if I have an appointment the way all those secretaries in New York City do. "He won't know my name but it's Lauren Laurano."

She nods and walks through a doorway to the back. I wonder if Latham is actually doing the baking. It seems unlikely. Still, I know in small towns like this the mayor usually doubles as something else. But even though he owns this place he probably has a baker working for him.

The woman returns. "He says he'll be right out," and gives an involuntary shrug as if to say I shouldn't count on it.

I try not to look at the goods. Impossible. There's a walnut brownie that particularly fascinates me. To take my mind off the chocolate I count the pieces of nut I can see and am deep into this pursuit when I hear a man's voice.

"Help you?"

The man behind the counter is the same one who an-
nounced Moffat's death in the deli, so he's obviously Luke
Latham. He has a long sharp nose like a fishing lure and
weak blue eyes. He wears a baker's apron but no hat; his
red hair clashes with the color of his face. I'd guess he has a
cocktail now and then.

I introduce myself and ask him if there's somewhere we
can go to talk. He stares at me, squints his already narrow
eyes, worries his lower lip with longish front teeth. Bugs
Bunny comes to mind.

"What's this about?"

"I'm investigating a crime."

"What's it got to do with me?" He acts alarmed.

"You *are* the mayor, aren't you?"

"So?"

"Well, this happened in your town."

"What did?"

"The death of Bill Moffat."

He exhales. Relieved. "That was suicide."

"I think that that remains to be seen."

Latham gives a bark of laughter. "Hanging? You think we
lynch people around here? You're not from these parts, are
you."

How do they always know?

"I've been hired by a local," I explain, as though this will
give me some sort of cachet.

It doesn't. He says, "Look, miss, I'm pretty busy and I don't
know that I've time for this."

"Mayor Latham, I'd think you'd want any doubts cleared
up."

"Who has doubts besides your so-called employer, which
I can guess who it is."

"Is there somewhere private where we can talk?" I ask
again.

More gnawing at his lower lip.

"C'mon back," he says, gesturing for me to come around
the counter.

I do and follow him through the door. There's a small office with two chairs and another door that leads to an area where I assume the ovens are. The smell is more pungent here and the room is warmer. He thrusts out a short arm with a small hand toward a rickety wooden chair. The seat is split so I sit carefully, adjusting my weight to avoid the crack.

"So?"

"How well did you know the deceased?"

"Moffat? We went to high school together. We didn't socialize now or anything like that."

"Where do you stand on fast food?"

"What?"

"Fast food. How do you feel about it coming up here onto your Fork."

"Progress is important. We need the jobs for our children and such. Look, you want my position on things you could get the minutes of meetings." He pulls on his nose.

"I like the personal touch," I say.

"Yeah, well." He indicates a bunch of papers spread out across his desk.

"I know you're busy, Mr. Mayor. But this is important."

"You going to ask me where I was when he died?" He gives me what passes for a grin. It's frightening.

"Should I?"

"You're the detective."

"Where were you?"

"How do I know? I don't know when he died."

Pretty good. I don't believe for a second that the mayor killed Moffat but I'm not convinced he doesn't know anything about it. I go back to my agenda. "So you're with the FEAG people then?"

"Did I say that? Huh? Did I? I said nothing about FEAG. They're a bunch of nuts like the AFF people. Folks should take stuff as it comes, that's the best way to go. Progress has always progressed."

I think of asking if I can quote him but hold the sarcasm. I'm afraid it would be lost on Latham anyway.

He goes on. "This is what I hate about you media people, always getting everything wrong."

"I'm not a media person, Mayor."

"Detective, media, what's the difference?"

Is he simply dumb or is this an act?

"I had nothing to do with Moffat or those groups or anything. Far as I can tell this whole thing is a personal suicide. You look into his personal life?" He raises both thin eyebrows. "You know about his, um, the women and such?"

I ignore his question, do a quick shift to throw him off balance. "What do you know about the death of Moffat's daughter?"

He doesn't blink. "Accident."

"Was it?"

"Fell off a bluff." Now he blinks. Rapidly.

"And what about the Silk Scarf killer, Mayor?"

His already red face flushes, then quickly pales. "In case you didn't know, that's being worked on. What's that got to do with Moffat?"

"I don't know. I'm interested in all of it. In my business you never know what might connect."

"Your business," he sniggers. "How come you don't do something decent with your life."

I want to smack him. "There's nothing indecent about what I'm doing, Mayor. I look for the truth. Something wrong with that?"

"Ah, you people wouldn't know the truth if you fell over it."

I have to assume he has a brain. "And what about the death of the Kemplers' child?"

"What are you driving at?"

"I think it's obvious, Mayor."

"Maybe to someone like you."

"Like me? What does that mean?" My homophobia antenna is up.

"A person who wallows around in the dirt all the time. The dirt of other people's lives."

Why do people view us this way? I suppose there's some

truth to it, but for me, it's like solving a puzzle. What I do is not that different from what Kip does. Or what a writer does. We uncover layers of lies and find reality. But the public views us as muck miners. Perhaps films and books — maybe even some in the business — have given us a bad rep. It's one of those things I have to contend with on every job but I never get used to it. I can't engage on this level.

"Mayor, could you tell me about the Kemplers' child?"

"Hit-and-run. Judy Kempler probably killed herself in despair."

"Two suicides in one week? Anyway, I thought it was clear she was a Silk Scarf victim."

"Clear? Clear from who?" His little rat eyes dart from place to place around the room.

"I have my sources," I say, enigmatically.

"Listen, you don't know anything about it, so why don't you go back where you came from which is probably New York City."

Another slur as he pronounces the name of my home with contempt.

"Are you saying that Judy Kempler wasn't murdered?"

He stands up. "I'm saying this interview is finished."

I rise. "Well, I thank you for your cooperation."

He nods, the irony lost on him.

Back in my car I think about what he's said and not said. Why was he so hostile? I don't believe it was because I was a stranger or that he has a deep-seated loathing for detectives. I feel he knows something, something he doesn't want to talk about, something that a lot of people know and don't want to talk about. Call me crazy, but I don't think it has to do with fast food.

Nineteen

Luke Latham sat in a booth at the Paradise waiting for some of the others. He'd been there three minutes and Millie hadn't taken his order yet. It pissed him off. What's the point of being mayor if you can't even get a dumb waitress to show you a little respect? And it wasn't like the place was packed or anything. Millie was behind the counter washing glasses or some damn thing.

He drummed his fingers on the Formica. He would've rather met over at Cubbie's Bar but he knew it was too early for the rest of them and he didn't want to give them any more to think about than they already had. It wasn't like he was an alcoholic or anything, but sometimes a guy wants a drink before five, so people get the wrong idea.

Finally, Millie made her way over to his table.

"Sorry, Mayor, didn't see you come in."

Latham knew she was lying, the fat slug. "That's okay, Millie, I know you were busy." He gave her his most sincere smile. She was a voter, after all.

"Want something besides coffee?"

"Got any Danishes left?"

"Apricot or prune."

He ordered the apricot. Thinking about that girl who came to see him, that detective or whatever, he almost laughed out loud except it wasn't that funny. She was funny, but not the fact that somebody got her here. Now they had a situation. Outsiders.

Millie put his coffee and Danish down in front of him and he thanked her. He remembered to thank everybody, no matter who. He had to think of reelection all the time. Pain in the ass.

Latham took a bite of the Danish and the apricot squirted out over his fingers. He swore softly to himself and sucked it off, then wiped the sticky remains with a napkin.

The thing was, he never wanted to be involved in this deal in the first place. Not that he really *was* involved. Looking the other way, was all. If anything got out, that would make him an accessory, wouldn't it? But who the hell knew things would go so far? When it first started it was no big deal. Well, it was sort of something, and the money was great. Nobody ever said anything about killings. Even now he wasn't sure of that. Still, coincidence goes just so far. The best bet for him was to get out of this mess. But would they let him? He swallowed hard. What happened to people who knew too much, knew even the little he was sure of? He didn't trust any of them.

He took another bite of the Danish and the same damn thing happened, only this time the apricot was dripping down his chin as Chief Wagner sat down opposite him.

Twenty

Lunch break.

The four of us sit on the floor in the middle of what might end up as a living room. The sandwiches are from the local deli in Seaview and aren't bad. I mean, they're not on focaccia bread but there's less fat in this so who cares?

I've decided it's best to *ask* about Annette and Cecchi rather than tell.

Jenny says, "Do they have any animals?"

"No."

"This is getting involved, isn't it?" asks Jill.

"I don't see what's so involved. I thought it might be good for Cecchi, that's all."

Jill says, "You mean it's turning into a big number?"

"I think it's more complex than I originally thought."

"Not FIG people," says Jenny.

"FEAG. No. Maybe. But I don't think so." It's not wise to tell them a serial killer might be on the loose right after they've bought a house here.

"Why do you need Cecchi's help to solve a hanging, even if it's murder rather than suicide?" says Jenny.

Kip gives me a knowing look.

"Sometimes you ask too many questions," I say.

"Oh, please. You sound like you're talking to children or something," Jill sneers.

"Yeah. Give," says Jenny.

I feel at a loss as to how to handle this. I know I have to

tell them something. "I think Moffat's death may be tied up with another murder."

"Another murder?" Both.

"I knew we shouldn't have bought this house, Jill."

"It has nothing to do with us."

"We don't have two murders where we live in Manhattan," Jenny says sensibly. "It's only two, right?"

Oh, boy. "Look, you know I can't go into all this."

"Since when?" Jill asks.

This is true. I've always told them everything about my cases.

"Since now. I don't know enough yet to go into it."

Jenny says, "But you know enough to want Cecchi out here to help you."

"If none of you minds."

They look at each other, shrug. "It's okay with me," Jill says.

The others agree.

Thank God. "I'll ask him then."

"Why don't you call him now."

I pretend to look around for a phone. "No phone."

"Try your purse," Jenny says.

"Can't get used to it." I laugh.

"Lauren, we know you've already asked him," Kip says.

"We do?" Jenny asks.

"I do. You have, haven't you?"

"Would I do a thing like that without consulting every-body?"

"YES." All.

To admit or not to admit? "I had to. I knew you'd be reasonable about it."

"If you knew that why didn't you ask first?"

"Time."

"Oh, hell," Kip says. "What's the difference."

Again they agree.

"When are they coming?"

"That I really don't know, but I think probably tomorrow. I have to check back with him."

"We'd better do a shopping later."

I say, "We don't have to fuss. Anyway, Annette has offered to cook."

Three pairs of eyes light up.

"This is sounding better," says Jill.

"I like it," Jenny says.

"And the shopping?" asks the practical one.

"It sort of goes together, don't you think? I mean, she'll shop for what she wants to cook."

"Good."

The Js seem to have forgotten about the case and I'm relieved we don't have to go on with that conversation. Eventually they'll find out but I'll deal with it then.

We gather up our garbage and stuff it into a plastic bag that Jill holds out. They're going back to their manual labor. I have to do more interviews. We say our good-byes and I promise to be home in time for dinner.

There are two ways to get to the South Fork. You can go through Riverhead and drive around, or you can take two ferries separated by Shelter Island. The first ferry is the one you see from the Js'. I decide to go this way and come back the other.

Because it's winter there's no line for the ferry and I wait in my car as it approaches from Shelter Island. When it lands and the gate is opened one car comes off. Then the ferryman motions me to come aboard. I get to park at the front. It's only a few minutes before we take off.

The ferry is small, unlike the one you take to get to Connecticut. Even though it's cold I get out of the Jeep and stand next to the railing. I watch as we pull out of the Seaview harbor, and the buildings grow smaller. I have to admit I like this, and the harbor looks cute. It might be nice to live here. Am I losing it?

The steely wind whips around me, my hair flying in all directions. It becomes too cold and I get back in the Jeep. The ticket seller comes to my window. I power it down. I'm shocked at the price. I didn't expect it to cost this much. I pay and buzz the window closed. Being up so high in the Jeep I can see everything. The Shelter Island shore is coming into view and the houses grow larger.

The ferry bumps the sides of the dock as the helper ties it up. The ferryman waves to me and I wave back, then realize he is only gesturing as to how I should drive. I'm the first one off. Actually, I'm the only one.

The first houses I see are ornate, adorned with ginger-bread moldings. I love them but I can't imagine what it would be like to live here, to be kept prisoner by a ferry schedule. And what could it be like to grow up here?

The road winds around through the island but it's easy to follow. I end up at another dock, ready to take the next ferry. When it arrives I see that it's about the same size as the first but can tell the ride will be shorter so I'm even more shocked when I buy my ticket and the price is so high. Again the ride is lovely, and when I get to the other side I ask directions, which are given to me in a taciturn manner and are easy to follow.

Southedges is one of the posh towns with old money. But as in almost any town, there's another part to it. This place is no exception. I drive to the street where Mary Lavin lived, one of the children whose names were given to me by Toby Moffat. The address turns out to be a trailer, yellow and blue, rusted and sagging. Why am I so lucky I don't have to live like this?

I park, walk up to the yellow door, knock a few times, and a hollow sound emanates from inside. I think back to another trailer, another case. Does it mean anything that trailers figure in my cases?

Decades pass before the door is opened. A large woman with red hair piled on her head in a haphazard way, a sanguine face, and drained brown eyes looks back at me. "Yes?"

I tell her who I am and after establishing that she's Ella Lavin, Mary's mother, I explain I've come to talk about her daughter.

"But why?"

"I think her death might be connected to others. I have no authority to question you so you don't have to speak to me if you don't want to. But Mary's death hasn't ever been properly solved, has it?"

"It was an accident."

"Was it?"

A look passes over her face, as though she's twisting this round and round, like clothes in a washer. I know it's not because she's never thought this before but rather the thrilling knowledge that someone else agrees with her. She steps back and lets me in.

Inside, the place is as pitiful as the outside. Sticks and stumps of furniture. She ushers me to a chipped plastic table with metal folding chairs.

"Tea? You want some tea? I'm having some."

"Thanks." I don't really want it but feel it would offend her if I refused.

She goes to the hot plate, pours me a mug, returns to the table, and takes a seat opposite. My mug is tan and has FILM FESTIVAL 1990 in green on it. I doubt that Mrs. Lavin got it at the festival. Ella is dressed in an aqua sweatshirt and purple sweatpants. They're clean and neat.

"So what do you have to say about my Mary?"

"I have a feeling you don't believe it was an accident."

"That's neither here nor there, young lady. You came here, you tell me what you know."

"I don't *know* anything. I have a feeling, that's all."

"That it wasn't an accident?"

"Right. I don't even know how she died."

Ella winces. "Fell down an old well. Hadn't been used for ages."

All of these deaths could've been accidents. Falling off a bluff; down a well; hit by a car. And could've been murder. Pushed, thrown, hit.

"How old was Mary?"

"Eight, poor baby."

"There have been others, Mrs. Lavin. Other children

who've died in what appeared to be accidents but could've been something else."

"Something else?"

I loathe to say the word to her. "Murder."

Her eyes light with acceptance. "Yes. Murder."

"Is that what you think happened to Mary?"

"It is."

"And do you know who did it?"

She tugs at a rogue hair that hangs down her neck. "No, I don't."

"Why do you think it was murder?"

"Because Mary knew about that well. From the time she could talk, was out and about on her own, playing, she knew. I stressed it, like. She wouldn't never have gone anywheres near it. I told the cops that but no one listened. Said I was refusing to accept the truth. I think it was them refusing to accept the truth." She takes a long slug of her tea as though her speech had dried up her throat.

"Before this happened, had Mary told you anything about strangers approaching her or anything out of the ordinary?"

"Nothing. But she was acting funny for about a month."

"What do you mean, funny?"

"It's hard to spell out. Was like she wasn't herself," Ella says, then eyes the tin ceiling like she's searching for a better way to say this.

"In what way?"

"Twitchy, like. All nervy. That wasn't like my girl. Mary was always laughing and happy, careless."

"And that month preceding her death she acted like she had something on her mind?"

"You could say that. A secret maybe."

"Did you ask her about it?"

"Sure. But she wouldn't tell me nothing. Said there wasn't nothing. But a mother knows. You got kids?"

"No."

"Sorry," she says.

"No, it's fine with me."

Ella looks at me as though I'm from another planet. "Fine?"

"Not everybody should have them," I try.

"Yer hubby? He feels the same?"

Why is there always this moment? I don't think this is the time to enlighten Ella Lavin. "We agree."

"Huh. I only had Mary 'cause I had the operation right after I birthed her."

"A hysterectomy?"

"That's the one. So now I don't have no kids." Her eyes fill and then she glances at me with a quick, dark, accusing look that says *You could have them if you wanted and you don't.*

"Not everybody is meant to be a mother," I feel the need to say again.

She gives me a curt nod, as though she agrees, but I know she doesn't. I have to get on with this. It's not my fault that Ella doesn't have other children.

"So you think Mary had a secret?"

"Yes. I didn't find nothing when I looked through her few things, after."

"Mrs. Lavin, do you have a husband?"

She screws up her face in distaste. "I do."

"I assume you talked this over with him and he couldn't come up with anything either?"

"You assume right. He couldn't come up with nothing about nothing ever," she says, derisively. "He's a boozer."

I nod with understanding. "So, that's it then. You don't have any ideas, any little thing, even if you don't think it's important?"

She shakes her head and I rise. "Can I leave you a phone number where you can reach me if you think of anything?" She says I can, and I do. We say good-bye.

Out in the Jeep I feel I've accomplished one thing. I believe in Ella's feeling that her child was murdered. Now I have to see why the Southedges police didn't believe her.

Twenty-One

I drive back from the South Fork by going through River-head. It's shorter and doesn't cost anything, but it's certainly not as picturesque.

I analyze my interview with the Southedges police chief and have to recognize that the man didn't know anything (unlike Chief Wagner in Seaview). This one honestly believes Mary Lavin accidentally fell down the well, and hell, maybe he's right.

Part of me feels I've gone off on some crazy tangent here, wigged out because I don't want to deal with something, though I'm not sure what. I have to get back to my original investigation. After all, I'm being paid to find out what happened to Bill Moffat.

Cecchi and Annette are coming out tonight. It'll be good to see them. A voice in my head asks me why I *really* want them here. I hate that little voice. The thing about it, the voice, is that it's usually so much smarter than I am. I suppose that's why I loathe it so.

Why do I want them here? For the reasons that are obvious. I need Cecchi's help and I think it would be good for him. What else?

I need more diversion from Kip.

What the hell does that mean?

I have a lot of diversions and why should I need more? Let's face it, our relationship has never quite recovered from . . . no, not Alex, which is what I think first . . . lots of things.

It isn't what it used to be. But what is? And would I want it back the way it was?

There were some wonderful things and there were plenty of not-so-terrific factors. We glided over our problems, made jokes, looked the other way. Why did I disappear into my computer, as Kip accuses me of doing? And why did she simply vanish? Was it her brother's death, as I thought? Is our relationship still viable? Oh, God.

The thought of being without Kip frightens and saddens me so much. We're tense and the fun has gone out of our couplehood. But should we stay together if we're not happy? Aren't we happy?

I can't deal with these questions now. They're too overwhelming, too dismaying and distracting. I have to concentrate on the case.

Yeah, sure.

A plume of frosty air shoots from my mouth like a puff of smoke when I get out of the Jeep on Sixth Street in Seaview. I glance toward the sky. Again it has that silver-gray look that precedes snow. I pray that it won't as it'll only make life more difficult, and the Cecchis might have a hard time getting here.

I have some trepidation about questioning Sonny Kempler the day after his wife has been murdered, but I need to try. Now *I* feel as though I'm in a horrible business. A sleazeball, the way everyone thinks of private eyes. And here I am again, not working on the Moffat case.

I go up the walk, ring the front bell of Sonny's house, a Victorian. A young woman in her twenties answers. Her clothes are a heavy red hand-knit sweater and black leggings with short black boots. She has long bleached-blond hair and the face of a hurt puppy. I tell her who I am and ask for Kempler.

She looks at me with contempt. "He's grieving, you know."

I nod. "I can imagine," I say, and stand my ground. "You are . . . ?"

Her lips press together while she thinks, as though she has to search to remember who she is. "A friend," she finally says, still obviously unable to come up with her name.

"Could you ask him if he'll talk with me?"

"Yeah, I could do that." She closes the door in my face.

How many doors have been shut this way during my illustrious career? Maybe I'm pond scum. Most people don't get doors shut in their faces.

She comes back. "Okay, he'll talk."

They always do, and I wonder why this is too.

I enter the front hall. She leads me to a living room where a man, eyes down, sits slumped at the end of an orange slipcovered couch.

"Here she is, Sonny."

He looks up slowly. He has a mildly mottled face, with a mustache like out-of-control vines. Brown eyes droop with the weight of sadness.

"Mr. Kempler, I'm so sorry about your wife."

"Are you?"

"Yes," I say honestly, "I am."

He nods like the bobbin on a fishing pole. "Yeah, okay." Kempler wears jeans and a gray sweatshirt, yellow work boots. "Sit down. Courtney, you wanna get us a drink or something?"

Courtney looks at me, waiting for an order.

"No, nothing, thanks."

"I'll have a beer," he says.

"Ya had two already, Sonny."

"What? You're keeping track?"

She sighs dramatically, leaves the room, presumably to get the beer.

"My cousin," he explains. "Means well, but she don't get it."

I can't help wondering if she's a cousin or a girlfriend. More sleaze thinking.

"You're in a lot of pain," I say.

He almost lights up with the knowledge that someone

understands. "Yeah, that's right. My kid died too. Before. Less than a month ago."

"I know. I wanted to talk to you about that."

"My kid?"

"Yes. If you can."

"Yeah. I can talk about it but I don't know if I can take it. Live with it all."

Is he threatening suicide?

"But I got Josey, my girl, to think of. My other girl, Bebe, is the one that had died."

"Bebe. How old was she?"

"Nine. Josey's eight."

Nine. They're all around the same age. "I know Bebe was killed by a hit-and-run. They find the driver?"

"Not yet. Chief says they're still lookin'."

Courtney comes back with a bottle of beer and a glass. "Here," she says gruffly.

He takes the beer from her, nods a thank-you. She leaves. I watch as he pours it carefully, tipping the glass to the side so he doesn't get too much of a head. After he takes a sip he wipes his crazy mustache with the back of his hand, though there's nothing on it.

"Kid killed. Wife killed. Too much, you know?"

"Your wife, how was she taking the loss of your daughter?"

"You kiddin'? She was round the bend, almost. Kept saying it wasn't an accident."

My detective's heart gives a cymbal crash. "Why's that?"

"You wanna know what I think?"

"Yes."

"Grief."

"What did she say? Why'd she say she thought it wasn't an accident?"

" 'Cause a some stuff Bebe had told her."

"Like what?"

"Bullshit. Kids make up stuff."

"Tell me anyway."

"Nah."

I want to shake him. "Please, it might be important."

"For what?"

How do I answer this? "My investigation," I try.

"What're you investigatin' again?"

"Bill Moffat's death," I answer truthfully, and know it makes no sense here.

But Kempler nods as though it's the most logical thing he's ever heard. "Yah, well. Bebe didn't even know Bill Moffat."

"Did Judy know Bill Moffat?"

"Yeah. We both knew him, slight."

"Then it could be important, see?" Totally bogus but in his state he believes and nods.

"Okay. Well, Bebe told Judy a buncha men took her to a shack or somethin' like that there. Said they done things to her. Judy believed her but I didn't. Old Beeb had a imagination. You shoulda seen her notebooks, fulla stuff. Judy said this was different."

Judy, I'm sure, was right.

"Did she do anything about it, your wife?"

"Yeah, she went to see Wagner, chief of police."

"And what happened?"

"He set her straight. Told her Bebe was making things up, but he'd look into it. I saw him next day and we had a good laugh. Now it seems like I'll never laugh again."

I know the feeling. "There's been a lot of documentation about kids not making up stuff like that."

"Documentation?"

Why am I bothering with this line of explanation? "Did Bebe mention any names?"

"Don't think so. No."

"But this is a small town, wouldn't she have known the men?"

"See, this is my meaning. She probably would. So why didn't she tell Judy who these so-called men were?"

"Did you talk to Bebe about it?"

He takes a long swallow from the bottle. The empty glass remains on the table. His face is slightly flushed. "Couldn't talk to my daughter 'bout stuff like that, hell. Anyways, I didn't believe it, like I told you."

"And why do you think Judy was killed?"

"*Why?* What do you mean, *why?*"

It does seem like a stupid question. "I mean, do you think there was any connection to what Bebe said?"

"How could there be?"

"You said Judy believed Bebe, went to the police. Is it possible the men who took Bebe to the shack —"

He jumps up. "No men took Bebe nowheres. I think you'd better go."

Is it because he believes this, or something else? But what could it be? The man has lost his wife and child. I have to remember how bereft he must be.

"I'm sorry, Mr. Kempler. Forgive me. Do you think your wife was murdered by this Silk Scarf killer, then?"

"Yeah, who else? And you know what? I'm gettin' some other people on this. No one's doin' nothin' out here. No one had never even heard about it, know what I mean? I'm goin' to call the big papers, get them to come out here, see what's what."

Oh, boy. Will he actually do this?

"We got a serial killer here and you wouldn't never know it."

I have to agree with him. At least that there's been little coverage. Does that mean I don't think there's a serial killer? I'm not sure. It looks like there's one, but something about it, something that connects these killings to the deaths of the children, makes me feel it's something else. And does it have anything to do with Moffat? It could. His child died, too. All in all there are too many deaths, accidental, murder, suicide . . . too many for them not to be connected somehow.

I reassure Kempler that I'll do whatever I can to help, give him my sympathy once more, and leave him to his anger, grief, and beer.

Outside it's dark. Night comes early in the winter and

there are no big city lights to make it feel friendlier. As I walk to my car I sense there are eyes on me but dismiss this as a paranoid thought by someone who is more afraid of the country than the city. Still.

When I get in the Jeep I lock it and feel safer. Is it an illusion? I don't stick around to find out.

Twenty-Two

Cecchi tells us, "The city's like a zoo lately. I mean, I knew that, but now me with nothing much to do, walking around on my own, I see it differently."

"We're not moving," Annette says.

We sit at the table having dessert and coffee. It's so good to have the Cecchis here. He looks better than he has since he was shot. Thinner than usual, he still has the same craggy good looks, his sad brown eyes a little more melancholy. He wears a navy turtleneck sweater and gray cords.

Annette is as attractive as ever. She's tiny, with the body of a dancer, which she was once. Her eyes shine like pieces of cobalt. She wears a purple jumpsuit with a lavender turtleneck beneath. I can never look at her now without remembering that Cecchi told me she'd once had an affair during their marriage.

When Kip found out about Alex and me I wanted to use the Cecchis as an example of a couple that weathered the affair storm, but I couldn't betray his confidence.

"It seems like everyone's moving out of New York," Jenny says.

"Who's everyone?" I ask.

She shrugs.

Annette says, "I grew up in a small town and I never want to live in another one."

"I had to beg to get her here," says Cecchi.

I know this isn't quite the truth.

"Wide-open spaces make me feel claustrophobic," Annette says.

We all laugh at the incongruity.

Everyone is finished so we leave the table. Since Annette cooked and I served, Kip and Jill do the clearing up and washing. Annette watches TV. Cecchi, Jenny, and I sit in the living room.

"Can I listen?" Jenny asks. She knows I'm going to fill him in on the case now.

Cecchi and I look at each other.

"It's okay with me," he says.

At first I'm worried, because of the serial killer, but I know what will happen, so I agree. I start with the hanging death of Bill Moffat. In the middle Jenny rises and says, "I don't get it. I'm going to read."

Right again!

When she's gone Cecchi says to me, "What's to get?"

"She has a block when it comes to murder. I don't know why she wanted to listen in the first place. Anyway, let me continue." And I do, ending with my Sonny Kempler interview that afternoon.

Cecchi raises his full eyebrows. "Quite a saga."

"What do you think?"

"About which part?"

"Well, first, do you think they're connected?"

"I do. I don't know why but I do. On the surface the Moffat hanging doesn't seem to have anything to do with anything. Can't even say why I think it's a murder but my gut tells me, hey, this whole thing is one thing."

"Good. That's the way I feel. Where should we start?"

As he's about to answer, the others come in from the kitchen.

Jill says, "We're going to let the animals out now."

Oh, boy. I look at Kip, who appears on the verge of a stroke. She's been dreading this moment since we arrived. Theo, Nick, and Nora haven't been in the same room together yet, but tonight's the night.

"I'm not sure we should subject Annette and Cecchi to this," Kip says in desperation.

"What're we being subjected to?" he asks.

Jill explains.

"We don't mind," Annette says, turning off the TV.

"Nah."

I can see that Kip knows she's outnumbered and that the moment has arrived.

Jill calls Jenny, who comes out of their bedroom. "I guess what we have to decide is which animals come out first."

We go back and forth on this and finally decide that it's best if the cats are in the room first so they can get away if they want to when Theo is let out.

I open the door to our bedroom and in a few moments the two Persians saunter out, Nick with his bushy tail in the air and Nora looking slightly less sure of herself. We all watch, as though it's a show, while they check out the perimeters, the stairs, and each piece of furniture. Seven hours later it's time for Theo's entrance.

"God, I hate this," Kip says.

"We know."

"Whatever you do," says Jill, "don't interfere."

"But what if Theo tries to bite them?"

Jenny says, "Or Nick tries to scratch out Thee's eyes?"

"Right."

"That won't happen," Jill says.

I agree.

"But what if it does?"

"I'll deal with it," says Jill. "Okay?"

Kip doesn't look reassured but she nods her assent.

Jill goes to their bedroom and opens the door slowly. There's a crash and a blur as Theo races into the room like she's been caged for years. Nora jumps up on the table but Nick holds his ground and looks at Theo like she's the whirling dervish that she is. That's my boy!

"Oh, God," Kip cries.

I go to her. "It's okay. Relax."

"You have to be kidding," she says.

"Then be tense but watch."

Nora is safely out of reach, her eyes on Theo every moment. Nick sits watching, waiting, as Theo approaches. Tail wagging, she lowers the front of her body and inches toward Nick. He doesn't move a muscle.

"See," I say to Kip.

"This is worse than being on a Ferris wheel." One of Kip's most horrendous childhood experiences, by which she measures many things.

"Nothing's happening."

"But it's going to."

"No, it's not. Look how brave Nick is being."

"He's in shock."

I put an arm around her, laughing. "No."

"Yes. I can see it in his eyes."

"Kip, face it, Nick is a cool cat."

Meanwhile, Theo inches closer so that the two animals' noses are almost touching.

Nick twitches.

"Ohmigod," says Kip.

I feel her trying to move out of my grip. "Leave them alone."

"Did you see that? Did you?"

"Nothing happened."

"How can you say that?" Kip asks. "Nick is terrified."

Nick is unruffled. Trust me. Theo, on the other hand, is beside herself with joy and not only does her tail wag but the whole end part of her appears to be doing a Latin dance step. And now she barks.

Nick blinks.

Kip's knees buckle. "Oh, no, oh, God. Help. Somebody help."

"Get a grip," Jill says.

"Hey, Kip," Cecchi says, "it's okay. The little guy's holding his own."

Annette says, "I'm glad we don't have any animals."

The standoff goes on and on. Finally, Nick turns his back

and walks away, sits under a dining room chair. Nora has disappeared. Upstairs, I suspect. Theo still wants to play and occasionally goes over to Nick, looks at him through the rungs of the chair, barks, prances, gives up, and wanders off to investigate something else until the next try.

For the rest of the evening we chat uncomfortably because of Kip's nerves. And by the time we go to bed all the animals are sleeping in their own corners. Cecchi and I make plans to have breakfast out and continue our discussion tomorrow.

Nick purrs on the pillow behind my head while Nora subs as a foot warmer for Kip. I'm reading Carol Anshaw's new novel in which her lover disappears. Why does this seem like such a good idea? Kip is reading the latest biography of Virginia Woolf, and the waves of coldness that wash over me from her are more than chilling.

I put down the book. "What?"

She ignores me.

"Kip?"

She turns and gives me a stony look.

"I asked you, what?"

"Excuse me? You asked me what? What what?"

"You know what I mean."

She marks her place, closes the book. "If I knew what you meant I'd have answered you."

"You mean you heard me say 'what' and ignored me?"

"It didn't mean anything to me. *What* is not a sentence."

"Oh, are we going to have a grammar lesson now?"

"Lauren, stop it, will you?"

"Stop what?" Anshaw's book falls to my lap. My place is lost in more ways than one.

"I don't think this is working, do you?"

"You mean having the Cecchis here or . . ."

"I mean us. You and me."

I'm stunned. "Why do you say that? I can feel that you're upset with me but I didn't realize it was this bad."

She turns in the bed so she's facing me. "I know you think about her all the time."

I don't have to ask who she means. "No, you don't know that. And it's not true."

"Tell me you never think about her."

To lie or not? No point. "I can't tell you that."

"See."

"Kip, you said I think about her all the time and that's not true but I'd be lying if I said I *never* think about her. Of course I do."

"Well, I can't live with that."

"With what?"

"With you thinking about that woman."

"You're being ridiculous. How could I not think about her from time to time? I wouldn't be normal."

"Who ever told you you were normal?"

"Very funny. The thing is I don't think of her with lust or longing. I wonder how she is, how she's getting along."

"Are you trying to tell me that you haven't been in touch with her?"

"I *am* telling you that."

"No E-mail, nothing?"

"E-mail? With what? Oh, so that's why you didn't want me to bring my computer." The light dawns.

"That's not why. You know why. Anyway, don't try to turn this discussion into something else. So, have you been in touch with her?"

"No."

"Well, why not? If you're so concerned about her welfare why haven't you been in touch?"

"I didn't think it would be a good idea."

"Because it would start up." This is not a question but an accusation.

"No. Silence and distance seemed the right course to take now. Maybe we'll be friends one day, I don't know. It seems unlikely, given how you feel."

"But you'd like to be friends with her?"

I shrug because I'm not sure. "I don't know how much we have in common but I'd certainly like to be friendly."

"Well, we know one thing you have in common, don't we."

I flinch, feel like I've been slapped. "Dirty pool," I say.

"I couldn't resist."

"You know what, Kip? You could. You can. This kind of stuff is ugly and it doesn't get us anywhere."

"Where do we want to go?"

"I thought we were trying to work this out. Isn't that part of the reason we're here?"

"And look what you're doing. We came here to help the Js and have a kind of vacation and you've taken on a job."

"Kip, part of our problems are money ones. We can't go on with this inequity, this power thing."

"Power thing?"

"Don't act innocent. You know damn well that you having all the money puts you in a power position."

"I never think of it that way."

I'm not sure I believe this. "Even if you don't it's inherent. I need this job. I'll never make as much money as you, but I have to hold my own."

"We're getting away from the real problem. Her."

"What more can I say about Alex? I haven't been in touch and I don't intend to be in the near future. Or never, if that's what you want."

"Why are you putting it on me? Why isn't it what you want?"

"If I were to decide to get in touch with Alex it would be as a friend."

"I've never felt so far away from you," she says.

I reach out a hand. She hesitates, then takes it.

"We have to give this a chance," I say.

"Do you have to do this job?"

"There are women and children being murdered. I can't let it go now, Kip. Please try to understand."

She nods.

"And you'll know in your heart of hearts that the Alex thing is over?"

She looks deeply into my eyes. "Tell me again."

"It's over."

"Okay. I believe you."

She comes into my arms, snuggles close.

Why is it I don't believe *her*?

Twenty-Three

At the Big Bagel Deli I order a Route 48, which is a fried egg, bacon, and cheese on a roll. Cecchi gets a jelly dough-nut. We both have sixteen-ounce containers of coffee. Our table is in the middle of the room near a half wall. I face the door. We are stoking up before we go to Bill Moffat's funeral. Toby Moffat called me earlier and said she thought it might be a good thing for me to come back to her in-laws' place afterward. I told her about Cecchi and she said it was fine to bring him.

We've gone round and round on the threads of the cases and admit we're getting nowhere so give it up for the moment. I throw Cecchi a small curve.

"How long did it take you to forgive Annette after she had the affair?" His eyes reflect pain and I'm sorry to have caused this. "Never mind. Forget it."

"No. It's okay. I guess it took me a long time. Couple of years, maybe."

"That long?" I'm horrified.

"Trust. It was more about trust than forgiving, I think. Kip giving you problems?"

I tell him she is.

"Well, you can't blame her, Lauren."

I shouldn't be surprised that he's on her side. If only I could talk to Annette. "She won't let go of it. Whenever there's trouble she throws in Alex."

"Natural."

"Cecchi, can't you tell Annette that I know?"

"Absolutely not. That would be me breaking a trust then."

"But you did."

"So what? She doesn't know that."

Is that what trust is about then? Whether the other person knows what you've done or said? I think the bottom line is that trust relies a lot on what a person can get away with. Does this make me a cynic? So what's new?

"You have to build back her trust in you," he says.

"How?"

"Time. You're over that girl, aren't you?"

"Woman. Yes, I am."

"So," Cecchi says, "you got to give Kip a chance to recover. It hasn't been that long and she needs to know it isn't going to happen again."

"And telling her that isn't enough?"

"Annette told me and told me and even though I basically believed her, I had this nagging doubt that it could happen with somebody else, or she might see that guy again and it would start up."

"So you two simply rode it out."

"Right." A big blob of jelly drops onto his plate and he scoops it up with his finger, puts it in his mouth. I don't find this at all disgusting. Love is a funny thing.

I look at my watch. "We'd better go."

Cecchi and I stand outside, freezing. We watch as the people file into the Presbyterian church in Easthead. Cecchi knows none and I recognize only a few, whom I identify for him. There are Toby and her daughter, of course. The girl keeps her face against her mother, who guides her into the church. With them are two older people I assume are Bill's parents.

Chief Wagner is there and so is Mayor Latham. They both give me the cold shoulder. I'm surprised to see Lee Howard come walking toward me. He stops.

"Hello, there."

I introduce him to Cecchi.

"Didn't know you knew Bill Moffat," he says, doing something with his eyes that I guess is an attempt to twinkle, but which gives me the willies.

"Didn't know *you* did," I say.

He smiles. "Well, you wouldn't, would you? How'd you know him?"

"I know his wife," I say honestly and quickly.

"Oh, yeah. Toby. Funny, I thought you told me you didn't know anybody in town."

I think. "No, I don't believe I said that."

"Guess not. Well, it's colder than hell out here. See you inside. Nice to meet you, Mr. Cecchi."

Cecchi nods and when Howard's gone he looks at me. "See what you mean. That's one slick dude. I think he knows something about you, Lauren."

"Funny. I was thinking the same thing."

More people whom I don't recognize arrive, and then Stash Volinewski appears with Jean Ashton. I wonder if they're an item even though she's married.

They stop and I introduce them both to Cecchi.

"Sad day," Volinewski says.

We all agree.

Ashton motions me aside. "How come you haven't called?"

"I don't have anything to tell you. Although I think I will soon."

"You mean you might know who did it?"

"No. But there are other things."

"And I have something to tell you. I don't know why I haven't called you. I meant to."

"Could Mr. Cecchi and I meet with you this afternoon?"

She looks alarmed.

"He's my associate."

"I see. I'm going to the Moffats' after the interment."

"Yes, so are we."

"I don't think we should talk there, do you?"

"No."

"We'll have the most privacy at my place. How about three o'clock?" she says.

"Fine."

We rejoin Cecchi and Volinewski, make more small talk, and then they go into the church.

Alison is not present and my heart goes out to her. But maybe she's glad not to have to attend. Before we go in I see one more familiar face: Edith from the library.

She pulls me aside. "Did you see him? Did you go and meet him?"

"I did."

"And?"

"He's definitely strange."

She smiles as though she's been vindicated. "You'll get him, won't you?"

"Get him?"

"Prove he killed Connie."

"I don't know about that. That's not the case I'm working."

"You'll do it. I'm counting on you." She squeezes my arm and goes inside.

Oh, boy. My favorite thing, somebody counting on me when I have nothing to do with whatever is on their agenda.

Cecchi and I follow her in and take seats toward the back so we can keep our eyes on everyone. We're slightly handicapped because we don't know who should be here and who shouldn't. But Toby has promised to point out anyone she doesn't know, or anyone she thinks we should talk to.

Soft organ music plays and the casket is in front surrounded by flowers. The minister walks up to the pulpit.

It's noon by the time we pull up at the Moffats' house. The place is on the main street and it's huge. A large glassed-in room is on one side and a columned portico on the other. I wonder if the Moffats have always lived here. The houses on either side are of the same era and also grand. I think this must've once been the place to live if you had money.

Inside, an older black man in a white jacket and black

pants takes our coats. Why do I feel he hasn't been hired only for this occasion?

"Do you work for the Moffats?" I ask him.

"Yes, ma'am. Thirty-five years."

"What's your name?"

"Brown."

"You don't have a first name?"

"Brown's what they call me. Brown's my name. Excuse me." He moves away from us and takes the coats from the new people entering.

Cecchi looks at me. "Brown," he says softly and rolls his eyes.

We've entered a world neither of us knows, a world that barely exists anymore.

The living room is beautifully furnished although not to my taste. The pieces are antiques, large and heavy. The rugs are real Orientals. I can see through to the glassed-in room where an enormous spread is laid and a bartender stands behind another table. He is also black, but younger. Brown Jr., maybe.

"You want a drink?" I ask Cecchi.

"Think they'd have a beer in a place like this?"

"Might. Probably have anything anyone would want."

Toby comes up to us. "I'd like you to meet my in-laws," she says, surprising me.

She leads us over to the two people who'd come into the church with her and Lita. They sit together on a brocaded love seat, he with his hand over hers. We wait while some people finish speaking with them and then Toby introduces us.

Softly, Toby says, "This is the detective I told you about, Mother."

The woman eyes me carefully and then says, "Come into the library with us, please. We need to talk."

Twenty-Four

The library is filled with well-read volumes on cherry-wood shelves. Comfortable club chairs face a fireplace.

Mrs. Moffat says, "Pull over those chairs there."

They are straight-backed with brown leather seats and we all take one so that we sit with our backs to the quiescent fireplace and face the Moffats, who take the clubs.

Jane Moffat is a woman in her mid- to late seventies. She's frail, her legs lean like flower stalks. She wears a simple black dress with a single strand of pearls. Her hair is short and permanented, with a bluish cast to it. In her elegance she is of another age, outmoded.

There are deep, dark circles under red-rimmed eyes that have spent hours crying. She has a small straight nose and thin lips touched with a hint of color. Bits of powder are caught in her wrinkles and two pink circles mark her cheeks.

John Moffat is probably the same age as his wife. He has an amazing head of white hair, a widow's peak sharp as a lion's tooth. His brown eyes reflect their share of tears. He's a handsome man even with lines that carve up his face like miniature crisscrossing roads.

He wears a black suit, white shirt, and a black silk tie. His shoes are black oxfords, tied with perfect bows. I wonder if Brown did this for him.

"Miss Laurano," she begins, "my daughter-in-law tells me that you've been engaged to investigate our son's death. And that you can't say who your employer is."

"That's right."

She waves a dismissive hand. "Well, I probably can guess and it doesn't matter. The important thing is that someone other than our inept police department is looking into it. There is no way my son would have killed himself."

"A number of people share that view, Mrs. Moffat."

She nods, as if to say, any sensible person would. "Even though Billy did some things," she glances at Toby and then quickly back to me, "that might appear selfish, the truth is, my son was one of the most selfless people I've ever known. That might sound like a mother talking but you can ask almost anyone. I say 'almost' because he had enemies. Obviously." Her hands dance in her lap like butterfly wings.

"Billy had a sense of responsibility in the true spirit of the word," John Moffat says.

She nods with every word he utters. "The point is, a man like this isn't going to commit the selfish act of suicide. Leave his wife and child to fend for themselves. And knowing how hurt we were by the death of our eldest son . . . no, he wouldn't do that to us."

Cecchi says, "Mind if I ask something?"

"Not at all," she responds.

"When was the last time you saw him?"

John answers. "The day before."

"And how did he seem to you?"

"Well, that was odd because he did appear nervous and usually Billy was a calm man. Didn't you think he was nervous, John?"

"Agitated."

"Yes. Agitated."

"Did you ask him about it?"

The Moffats looked shocked, as if Cecchi had asked if Bill had mooned them.

"Why, no," she answers.

John shakes his head.

"Why not?"

Cecchi doesn't quite understand what kind of people these are.

"If he'd wanted to tell us he would have," John says.

"You have any ideas why he was so nervous?"

"Agitated," John repeats. "I hadn't seen him like that since Freddy died."

Jane Moffat says, "Oh, dear, it's been one tragedy after another. Whatever anyone else says I don't think this had to do with fast food. I know Billy was fighting that but as much as I agreed with him and detest those FEAG people, some of whom I've known for years, I can't imagine them doing something like this."

"So what do you think happened?" I ask.

"Well, he did say one thing to us another time, not that last time but about a week before." She looks to her husband to continue.

"He'd dropped by for a cocktail," John says. "Always had one martini, never more." He smiles fondly, then it disappears abruptly as he realizes that he'll never have another drink with his son. "We were talking about the area and how things had changed since Billy was a boy. People came up. I'm not exactly sure how to say this."

"Of course you are, dear," his wife interrupts. "Class. We were talking about the class of people who live here, run things now."

John appears slightly embarrassed, as though he knows this isn't politically correct while his wife doesn't. It's hard to believe either of them would know that.

"It was a discussion, not a judgment."

"Oh, John," she says and shakes her head.

"Well, anyway," he goes on, ignoring her. "Billy said the strangest thing. He said, 'You have no idea what you're saying.' I thought he was chastising me for some old-fashioned attitudes, but I found out that wasn't it when I questioned him further."

"No. Not at all," Mrs. Moffat adds.

"What *did* he mean?" I ask.

"He said no one is who you think they are. I told him I've known that for years and asked him who specifically. But all he would say was that he wasn't ready to go public yet. I pointed out that we were hardly the public and he laughed but said he needed more proof before he could say anything else."

"And that was it," Cecchi says.

Mrs. Moffat looks at him as though he's insane or worse. "What more could be said?"

"Well, ah, you didn't ask him . . . I don't know, who or what he was talking about?"

"Why would I do that?" John answers. "He'd already said he couldn't say more."

Cecchi and I aren't used to letting things go because someone tells us that's it, so it's hard to understand this attitude.

"But," I press on, "this thing he said, this came after you were talking about people around here. I believe you said 'people came up.' Who were these people?"

"Is that important?" she asks.

"It might be."

The Moffats exchange a look. Then she answers. "First, we were talking about regular people, citizens of the area. After a few moments of that it switched to persons in the local government."

"So Bill could've been referring to them?" Cecchi asks.

John says, "Yes. He could have. But it also could have been the others."

"I don't think so, John," she says. "I think it was the government people he meant."

"You mean the mayor and supervisor, people like that?" I ask.

"Yes. But he didn't say directly."

I wonder why she's so eager to protect them when she's called us in here to tell us this. "Nevertheless, one thing followed the other?"

"Yes."

Cecchi says, "Can you tell us the names of the people you were talking about?"

"As you said, we mentioned the major ones, mayor, supervisor, chief of police," John replies.

"The mayor and the supervisor. Humph. They're not exactly the types of people who used to run things around here," Jane Moffat says.

"We're not saying they're terrible people, we're saying they aren't of the caliber we had become accustomed to."

"But Bill said, 'No one is who you think they are,' and that came right after discussing these people?"

"Yes."

I can tell this is all we're going to get. I stand up and Cecchi follows suit. "You've been very helpful. Thank you."

They smile grimly and rise along with Toby.

"I guess we should go back to our guests," Mrs. Moffat says.

We follow them into the living room. I look around and see that the chief and mayor are here. I don't know who the supervisor is so I ask Toby.

"He's standing by the bar, see the one in the plaid suit?"

I do. "Will you introduce us?"

She agrees and we go into the glassed-in room where we are introduced to Supervisor Julian Perini. He's a large man with a stomach that hangs over his belt and hands the size of roast beefs. Perini's head is dome-shaped, the dark hair showing the teeth marks of his comb. He's eating something as he talks to us and it swirls inside his mouth as though it's in a Cuisinart.

"So you're the detectives. Lookin' into this suicide, thinkin' it's a murder, huh?"

We nod. I say, "I wonder if we could talk to you."

"I thought that's what we're doin'." And he laughs too loud and long for the so-called joke.

I wait it out. "A private appointment. When could we come to your office?"

"Busy, busy, busy. Call my secretary, set something up."

"I know you're busy but we need to do this fairly soon."

He reaches his meaty hand into his inside pocket and pulls out a brown leather cardholder, removes a card, and hands it to me. "Call my secretary."

I know I won't because she'll put us off. We'll show up. It's the most effective way and I've done it with the best. We shake hands and return to the living room, where I spot a frightened-looking Jean Ashton. A tall, gangly man stands next to her. She motions us over.

"This is my husband, Thomas, who's just come back from a business trip," she says pointedly.

We shake hands with Ashton.

After some small talk he says, "So what nitwit hired you to look into an obvious suicide?"

Neither Cecchi nor I look at Jean. "Not at liberty to tell you that, Mr. Ashton." It's clear by his attitude why she hasn't told him.

"Well, if some jerk wants to spend his hard-earned money on something as clear-cut as this it's no skin off your nose, is it?" Ashton gives a smarmy smile and his long face appears longer. "I'm getting a drink," he says. "Want one, Jean? Anybody?"

"Yes," she says, a desperate sound in her voice. When he's gone she turns to us. "I didn't expect him back until tonight. We can't go to the house. There's a diner in Pequash on the main road. Meet me there at three. Oh, God, this is awful."

Twenty-Five

Thomas Ashton was in a rage. He threw a scotch and water down his throat as though he was putting out a fire, told Jean he was going to his office, gave his condolences to the Moffats and Toby, then left.

Outside he got into his baby blue Mercedes SL and headed toward the town hall where he thought he'd wait for Perini. He knew damn well that Jean had hired those asshole detectives.

Jean had been saying all week that Billy hadn't killed himself and that the police would never do anything about it, so it wasn't that hard to figure out that she'd hired these dumbos. But that was the worry. Maybe they weren't so dumb. Maybe they'd dig up stuff; dig up trouble. One thing could lead to another and somebody might take an interest in him. What he did with his free time. Shit. If he'd known at the start where it would all go he wouldn't have gotten involved.

He pulled out a cigar from his pocket, maneuvered to get off the cellophane with his teeth, then bit off an end. He pushed in his lighter, waited, then when it popped out he lit up.

Was that true? Would he have said no if he knew then what he knew today? When it first came up it was one thing, but now it was turning into something else. The truth was it had been sour for a while, but he hadn't wanted to look at it. Pretended those other things weren't happening, had nothing to do with him.

Billy's death was different. He hadn't ever liked the asshole but he didn't want the sucker dead. Thing was, until Jean went and messed into it nobody would've given two farts, would've taken things at face value. But now. Jesus.

Tom parked across the street from the town hall. He never locked the car here, only in Seaview where there was another element. When he got out he pulled up his coat collar against the wind that was getting nastier by the minute and crossed the street.

Once inside, he went into the office that the board members shared, took off his coat, and hung it up. Then he sat down at the metal desk and punched in some numbers.

When Perini's secretary picked up he told her to buzz him when her boss came in. She said she would.

He sat back and waited and wondered. How long was it going to take before the others came barging in here, or into his office, and demanded to know how the hell he could let his wife hire those detectives? He was going to look like a pussy.

Christ Almighty, Jean had put him in deep shit.

Twenty-Six

It's begun to rain, the freezing kind that hits you like pellets. The sky is gray, leafless branches of trees against it, fingers from a horror film. A wicked wind takes swipes at us. We don't have an umbrella so we run to the car.

Inside we wipe our faces with tissues and shake ourselves like dogs.

I say to Cecchi, "So what do you make of that?"

"Which thing?"

"First the Moffats."

"Could you tell me why they didn't ask their own kid what the hell he was talking about?"

I smile. "I probably wouldn't know if I didn't live with Kip. The Moffats are WASPs."

"Kip's not like that."

"No, but her mother is and some of the rest of her family."

"You mean they think it's improper or something to ask questions?"

"Something like that."

He shakes his head, perplexed. "I don't get it but it doesn't matter. The thing is, from what you told me, and now this, it definitely sounds like Bill Moffat was on to something big."

"Definitely. 'No one is who you think they are.' I think he was talking about the movers and the shakers of this Fork, don't you?"

"Maybe some others, but the most respectable for sure."

"It wasn't suicide, Cecchi. It couldn't have been."

"I agree."

"So why are the police so eager to declare it that?"

"Saves a lot of work," he says cynically. "Nah. It's more than that. Maybe the cops are involved themselves."

"My thoughts exactly. But involved in what?"

Since we have to wait until three to see Jean Ashton, I suggest to Cecchi that we talk to Chief Wagner about the accusations that Bebe Kempler made.

Cecchi says, "A *bunch* of men, she said?"

"That's the way the father put it. We'll never know exactly. Let's see how Wagner characterizes it."

I start the Jeep.

Cecchi says, "And what about this Ashton guy? Why is the wife so afraid of him?"

"His attitude about us. I mean, after what he said I'm sure she doesn't want him to know *she's* the jerk who hired us."

"But she seemed nervous before he said that stuff."

"He'd probably already said something like it to her before introducing us," I say.

"Why introduce us at all?"

"Good question. Unless she wanted us to see what he was like, get to change the place where we were going to meet."

"She could've gotten us aside and changed the appointment. I think she wanted us to meet him."

"We'll ask her," I say.

"You mean it won't be improper to ask a question?" he says facetiously.

I laugh.

At police headquarters Sergeant Lockwood is ready for me.

"Chief's tied up," he says.

"So untie him," Cecchi says.

I give him a gentle kick. "Tell him we're here."

"Said he didn't want to be interrupted."

"Do it," Cecchi says.

"Who the hell do you think you are?" Lockwood asks.

"Peter Cecchi."

"Huh?"

I say, "Buzz him."

"Look, miss, I have instructions."

I feel sorry for Lockwood because I know he does have orders to follow. I think of all the secretaries in New York City whom I've outwitted and I wonder if any of those tactics would work here. I know where the chief's door is and I could probably make it there before Lockwood. It'll leave Cecchi standing alone but I can get him in afterward.

"Who's that?" I ask, and look over Lockwood's right shoulder. When he turns I make my dash for the door and get it open before he can stop me.

The chief, as I expected, is with no one, not even on the phone. He's sitting at his desk, feet up, playing with a Gameboy.

"What the hell?" he squawks. He drops his feet to the floor and tries to hide his toy.

"Winning?" I ask him.

Lockwood, with Cecchi right behind him, appears at the door. "Chief, I tried —"

"Get the hell out of here, Lockwood, you useless piece of . . . go on, get. What the bejesus do you want? And who the hell is that?" He points at Cecchi.

"This is my associate, Mr. Cecchi. He's working on the case with me."

"The case." Wagner sneers. "There is no goddamn case."

"We'd like to talk to you about Bebe Kempler."

"Who?"

I see recognition in his insincere eyes no matter what he says. But there's no advantage in accusing him of stalling or pretending. So I play my part.

"Bebe Kempler was the daughter of Judy, who, by the way, was murdered, and she claimed that some men had taken her somewhere and done things to her."

"Oh, Kempler," he says, as though I hadn't said the name correctly the first time. "The Kempler murder is being looked into, what are you talking about?"

"Which Kempler murder?" I ask, and take a chair, indicate that Cecchi should do the same.

Wagner is thrown by both the question and our making ourselves at home. "What do you mean, *which* Kempler murder?"

"Judy's or Bebe's?"

"Bebe's? That wasn't a murder."

"So you recall the little girl?"

"Hit-and-run," he says, ignoring my sarcasm.

"You find the driver?" Cecchi asks.

Wagner gives him a beady stare. "I don't remember."

"Guess you got a lot of cases to keep track of," Cecchi says. "Why don't you look it up?"

"You telling me how to do my job?"

"You haven't found the driver," I say, to defuse the situation.

"How do *you* know?"

"Sonny Kempler told me."

"What the hell you doing talking to him? What's going on here? That's a crime scene over there, you going in, messing it up? You people have no rights here. You say you're investigating Moffat's death and you're talking to Kempler. What's he got to do with Moffat? What's Bebe got to do with Moffat?"

The chief's face has become a shade of purple I've never seen and he's standing up, fists clenched at his sides.

Calmly, I say, "Why does this make you so mad, Chief? A person might think you have something to hide."

He squeezes his lips together, blinks rapidly as he stands there, speechless, undoubtedly weighing what I've said. In a low, controlled voice he says, "I have nothing to hide."

Cecchi says, "Then you won't mind answering some questions."

"What about?" He sits down, but his fists are still clenched as they rest on his desk.

"Bebe Kempler."

"I told you, that was a hit-and-run."

"Yes. You told us. But what about her claims that some men had abused her?"

"That was, whatchacallit, fantasy."

"Judy Kempler didn't think so."

"Yeah, well, Sonny did. These mothers get all hysterical, kid tells them something like that. It's a proven thing that these kids make up this malarkey."

"Really? Who proved that?" I ask.

"What?"

"You said it was a proven thing. Who proved it?"

"Now look," he says, beginning to appear apoplectic again. "Don't go twisting my words. The point is, the kid made it up and I told the mother."

"Actually," I say, "I think you told Judy Kempler you'd look into it."

"Well, so what if I did?"

"Did you? Look into it?"

"What the hell's wrong with you? Didn't you hear what I said? There was nothing to it. Nothing to look into. Where should I have looked, huh? This crazed woman comes in here, tells me some cock-and-bull story, no names, no places, what am I supposed to do with that? Huh? You tell me."

"Did she say you couldn't question Bebe?" I ask.

This stops him. He stares.

"Did you ask to question Bebe?" Cecchi says.

Nothing.

"Did it *occur* to you to question Bebe?"

"You don't question nine-year-old kids about disgusting stuff like that," he screams.

"Yeah, you do," Cecchi says, matter-of-factly.

"Is Judy Kempler's another Silk Scarf murder?"

"Hell, you know it is, you talked to Sonny."

"Sonny's going to call the New York City newspapers to come out here," I say.

"Where you get that?" Color drains from his face as though he's losing blood.

"Horse's mouth."

Cecchi says, "What kind of progress have you made on these Silk Scarf murders?"

"I want you people to leave," he says. "You got no right to

question me about Silk Scarf or Bebe Kempler or anything else."

He's correct about that. But what do rights have to do with it?

"So," Cecchi says, "let me get this straight. A mother comes in, gives you a complaint about her child being molested, and you do nothing? Is that what you're saying? Because if it is I think the C.O.L.D. should be told about this, don't you, Lauren?"

"Absolutely," I say, having no idea what those initials stand for.

"What's that?" Wagner asks. "What's the C.O.L.D.?"

Cecchi sniggers. "Boy, this is some kind of police department. A chief who doesn't even know what C.O.L.D. is." He stands up. "Let's go, Lauren. We're wasting our time here."

"No," Wagner says. "Wait."

We look at him.

"I didn't think there was anything to the complaint. I thought it would be worse to haul a little kid in here and question her, you can understand that, can't you?"

We look at him.

"Next day, Sonny comes in here and makes like it was all in the kid's mind. So what was the point?"

We look at him.

"If I'da had other complaints, well, then, sure I woulda done something about it. You can be sure of that. There's no reason to go to C.O.L.D. None at all. I do a good job here. Ask anybody."

I rise. "We will."

Cecchi and I head toward the door.

"Wait. You gonna report me or what?"

I open the door, turn back to him. "We'll see. Depends on what other people have to say. Right, Cecchi?"

"Right," he says.

And we leave.

Twenty-Seven

As we pull up to the Pequash Diner we're still laughing about C.O.L.D. Cecchi told me he felt a cold coming on and it was the first thing that came into his mind.

The diner is authentic-looking from the outside, like a train car. The trim has recently been painted red. It's still an amazing thing to me to get a parking place right in front of where you're going, like in 1940s movies about New York City. That kills me, when a car pulls up in front of an office building on Fifth Avenue and there's a perfect space. I guess this is one advantage to small-town living. Kip will be pleased when I mention it to her.

Cecchi and I have agreed that Chief Wagner is hiding something. What, is the question. Perhaps Jean Ashton will shed some new light.

The diner inside is like diners anywhere. Counter, stools, Formica-topped tables. We take a booth. There are two men in plaid shirts and winter vests at the counter, drinking coffee. Otherwise the place is empty.

A waitress with dyed hair that looks like an animal pelt asks us what we want.

"How are the brownies?"

"Homemade."

This does not necessarily mean good. Whose home, after all? "Nuts or no nuts?" I ask.

"Nuts."

"Chewy or soft?"

She puts a hand on her waist and leans to the side. "Say, what is this? You Martha Stupid Stewart or somebody? You want a brownie or not?"

"I like my brownies a certain way," I say timorously.

"The way we got them is good. Lena makes them herself."

Cecchi says, "Why didn't you say that right away. If Lena makes them then there's no problem, right, Lauren?"

"Had I but known," I say. "I'll have two."

The waitress lifts a perfectly tweezed eyebrow. "Two? You sure?"

"If Lena makes them then I have to have two."

She shrugs. "Okay, it's your funeral."

This doesn't bode well and I haven't a clue as to why she'd say this. But I decide not to ask. I add a coffee to my order and Cecchi gets the same, minus the brownies.

I say, "I think it's time we run a check on everybody involved."

"I'll call Detective Lent later."

"God, this is when I can't stand not having my computer. I hate Kip."

"No, you don't and she was right. Anyway, what could you do with it that would have any pertinence to this case?"

"That's not the point."

The waitress is back and now I understand completely why she said what she did. They are two of the biggest brownies I've ever seen. They hang over the sides of a dinner plate. I look up at her and she's smiling . . . no, smirking, as if to say, I dare you to finish them both. But, of course, she doesn't know who she's smirking at.

"They look delicious," I say.

"Would you expect less from Lena?" Cecchi says.

"Of course not."

The waitress looks from me to him then back. "You're going to eat them, aren't you?"

"Naturally."

"I'll believe it when I see it," she says and places our coffees in front of us.

"You have to, Lauren."

"But of course, dear boy. I have a reputation to up-hold."

"Kip would go crazy if she saw you eat that."

"Maybe. Maybe she wouldn't care anymore."

"Hey," he says, "don't —"

But this is when Jean Ashton walks into the restaurant. She hangs up her coat and I see that she's changed out of her dress into more casual clothes: pants, sweater, turtleneck. I move over so she can sit next to me.

"Thanks for meeting me here," she says.

"Sure. Easier for us."

She eyes my plate of brownies. "You *really* like chocolate, don't you."

I recall then that I'd eaten all her cupcakes. "I guess I'd have to call it an addiction," I say sheepishly.

"Mine's salt," she says. "Chips, pretzels, popcorn, any-thing with salt. We all have one. How about you, Mr. Cecchi?"

"Call me Cecchi. I guess work's my addiction. We were wondering what the problem was, why you wanted to meet here."

The waitress returns.

"Just coffee," Jean says. To us: "Well, you heard my husband's attitude."

Cecchi asks, "Was it a surprise to you?"

"No. The surprise was his return. I expected him to be away at least another day. He probably suspects it's me who hired you, but there's no reason to give him proof." She smiles.

I take a bite of the brownie. Ohmigod. It might be one of the great things in life.

"Why do you think he's so aggressively against your hir-ing us?"

"Maybe because he never liked Bill. Not that he would want to see him dead," she adds quickly. "Or maybe because he thinks I spend my money foolishly."

"*Your* money?"

"I inherited a great deal. Tom thinks he has a right to tell me how I can use it."

"But he has money of his own?" I ask. "Advertising?"

"Yes. But he spends more time at the town board than he does at his company."

"Why's that?"

"For one thing he's on the board. And I think he likes hanging out there with all the other members, I don't know. Why do men do anything they do? Sorry," she says to Cecchi.

"It's okay," I say. "Cecchi's not like regular men."

"Hey," he says.

"You know what I mean. The town board, I assume, is like it is in any area, part of the local government?"

"Yes. The councilmen, the trustees, that sort of thing."

This is what I thought. "Jean, both Cecchi and I got the feeling you wanted us to meet your husband for a particular reason."

She flushes slightly. Takes a swig of coffee, looks out the window. Now I know we were right.

"Jean?"

"Well, what did you think of him?"

Cecchi says, "Didn't get to talk to him."

"Still, you must've gotten an impression," she says sadly.

"He seems . . . angry," I say.

"Yes. He hasn't always been that way. He was different when we were first married." She says this in a dreamy way, as though longing for the good old days. Maybe no one can sustain a marriage, maybe it isn't natural for two people to stay together for years and years.

"Was that the only reason you wanted us to meet him?" Cecchi asks.

"No. Besides being angry all the time he's become secretive. I don't think he's having an affair, even though our sex life's been dead for years. But something's going on."

"Do you think it has to do with Bill? His death?"

"No. This started a long time ago . . . three or four years

back." Suddenly she changes, becomes almost perky. "But this isn't the reason I wanted to see you."

Something odd is going on here but I know that pressing her about her husband or her change in demeanor will get me nowhere. I make a mental note that Ashton needs a closer look.

"I've been meaning to call you since you were at my house. After you left I remembered something Bill said the last time I saw him. He said he thought someone was following him."

"Did he say who he thought it was?" Cecchi asks.

"He didn't know."

"Anything else?"

"No. That's the only thing I remembered."

"Was he afraid?"

"Afraid? He used the word 'uneasy.' "

Cecchi says, "Pretty cool customer. He thinks he's being followed and he's *uneasy?*"

"Perhaps he *was* afraid," Jean says. "It's the family way to understate things. I can't actually imagine Bill using the word *afraid*. I don't think it would be in his vocabulary."

"So then he might have been afraid?"

"Yes."

"Jean, did Bill ever talk to you about his daughter's death? I mean, did he ever say that he thought it wasn't an accident?" I ask.

She reels back slightly as though I'd slapped her. "God. I'd forgotten all about that."

My detective's heart does the Macarena. We wait for her to compose herself, get ready to tell us.

"It wasn't in that same conversation. But it wasn't that long ago either."

"What exactly did he say?"

"He said it was probably crazy but he was beginning to think Freddy's death wasn't accidental. When I asked him to elaborate he said he couldn't. There were things that were beginning to add up in a way that he didn't like, that made him think that. He said something else too, something I thought was off the wall."

"Which was?"

"He said he didn't think Freddy was the only one."

"The only child?"

"Yes."

Without hope I ask, "Did he name the others?"

"No. But he said there were four of them."

I'm startled. Four. I only know about three: Freddy, Mary Lavin, and Bebe Kempler. Who's the fourth?

"Jean, think hard. Did he say anything about the other children, anything that might give us a clue to their identity?"

A light comes into her eyes and I know she's recalled something.

"He did say one thing. He said three of them were white and one was black and that nobody even noticed her death, the black child. Bill was disgusted by the way blacks are treated here."

A black child. It shouldn't be too hard to find out who that was.

"You see," I say, "you had more information than you thought."

"Yes, but I didn't know that when I asked to meet with you."

I wonder why she didn't call. "I believe you, which makes me curious as to why you didn't phone me. Wouldn't it have been easier?"

The flush starts at her neck and travels upward until her blush is in full bloom.

"What is it?" I ask gently.

Her eyes are slightly glassy with the prospect of tears. We wait. Finally Jean Ashton says:

"This is hard to say. But, well, it was something to do."

My heart breaks for her. How terrible it must be to have a life so empty that meeting with a detective is an event. "I understand," I say quickly.

Cecchi clears his throat a few times. "Yeah. Me, too."

She tries to smile and it comes off lopsided. "Thank you," she whispers.

"Can you think of anything else, Jean?"

She shakes her head. "But if I do, I'll . . . I'll call you."

"We can meet," I say.

"Please," she says and I realize I might have sounded patronizing so I apologize.

We finish our coffee and I have consumed only one brownie. When the waitress comes over her smirk is gargantuan.

"Like a bag?" she asks me.

I hate her. "Yes, thank you. Tell Lena she makes one great brownie."

"She knows."

Outside we stand together and I see that Jean's extremely nervous. I know it's because she's afraid her husband might come by and see us together.

"You'd better go," I say.

She looks at her watch.

Looking past Jean I see Lee Howard from Vreeland's Motors come out of the pet store. He sees us too, but turns and walks the other way.

Jean says, "It's getting late. Have to get home and start dinner. Thank you for seeing me."

"Oh, no. Thank *you*. You've been extremely helpful."

"I hope so," she says, in a way that lets me know she's still embarrassed about her need for company.

We watch her hurry to her car and then we get in ours.

Cecchi says, "What do you think about Tom Ashton?"

"I think Jean had more to tell us but couldn't."

"Agreed. Maybe we can get it out of her another time."

"Maybe," I say.

"You didn't know about the black kid, huh?"

"No."

"We can look up deaths in the local paper," he says.

"I think we can find out an easier way."

Twenty-Eight

There's a gas station in Seaview near the street where the Js have their house that either is run by blacks or that has black employees. I've used it once since I've been here. Attached to it is a convenience store that looks like the place where pot was invented and seems to be peopled by rejects from certain talk-show audiences.

I don't need gas so I pull over into a parking space, and Cecchi and I get out of the car. A black man in his thirties is filling a green Dodge Shadow, the one with the gold stripe across its side and gold spokes in its wheels. Supposed to look sporty but doesn't. An old lady is in the driver's seat.

The attendant keeps eyeing us as we stand to the side waiting for him to finish. He's a good-looking man with mocha skin and deep brown eyes. He wears khaki pants, a tan parka, and a blue watch cap. He finishes filling the tank, makes the money exchange, and she drives off. He stands still, staring.

We walk over and I can tell he's thinking bad things about us. Worried that we're going to hassle him some way. I wonder why he thinks that?

I introduce myself and Cecchi, stick out my hand.

He looks at it like I have six fingers, then carefully accepts it, shakes gently. "I'm Claude Fry. Everone calls me Cloudy though. They couldn't get it right when I was little."

"Your sisters and brothers?"

"My teachers."

"Where you from, Cloudy?" Cecchi asks.

"Here."

Good. He'll know everything.

"I ain't done nothin'," he says.

"Didn't think you had. I want to ask you a few questions about a little girl."

"What little girl?"

"That's what I don't know. I thought you might be able to tell me or lead me to somebody who might know. You been around here the last four or five years?"

"Yeah."

"Know about any little girls who died during that time?"

"Died how?"

"Probably an accident," Cecchi says.

"You must be thinkin' 'bout Chantel then."

"Could be. How old was Chantel?"

"I think she was nine or ten, maybe."

"How'd she die?"

"Fire. That would be an accident, wouldn't it?"

"Could be. Was it a suspicious fire?"

"What you mean, suspicious?"

"Did anybody, the fire department, ever find out how the fire started?"

"You'd have to ask them. I don't recall hearing that, though. Maybe you should talk to her mama."

"I think you're right. Can you give me her name and address?"

"Sure can."

Back in the car Cecchi says, "That was racist, you know. Good work, but racist."

"What do you mean?"

"Thinking that all black people know each other."

"I think they do here."

"Racist."

"Call me David Duke." I guess he's probably right about it being racist but it *did* bring results and for the moment that's all I'm interested in.

When we turn off Main Street onto Lynette Drive the difference is immediate. The houses here are smaller and run-down. It's not about not caring for property but rather about being poor. We make a few turns until we're on Smith Street, where we slow to a crawl looking for number 450. We find it and park in front.

The house is a one-story with a cement block foundation. The facade is made of purple shingles, old and cracked. Cecchi and I take the cement steps to a small open porch and I knock on the door. In only moments the door is opened and a black woman stands before us.

"Mrs. Washington?" I ask.

She gives us the once-over. "Who want to know?"

"I'm a private investigator and this is my partner."

"What you investigating?"

"If you're Mrs. Washington we'd like to talk to you about the death of your daughter Chantel."

Her deep brown eyes change from suspicion to sorrow in an instant. "You show me some proof who you are?"

I produce my P.I. license. She doesn't press Cecchi for I.D. and stands aside to let us in.

"Come on into the kitchen."

We follow her down a hall and into a sunny room that is neat and clean though the furniture and walls show signs of age. There's a wooden table with four matching chairs and she urges us to sit down.

"Want coffee? I always got a pot going."

We both accept.

She pours us each a mug and puts milk in a small white pitcher on the table. The sugar bowl is already there. My mug says VEDA AND MONTY 1975 and Cecchi's THE HAMPTON CLASSICS. Mrs. Washington notices me reading them.

"Yard sale," she says.

I smile, nod. She brings over her own mug which says ONE DAY AT A TIME and sits down.

"What you mean you investigating about Chantel? It's more than a year and nobody done any investigating before."

I feel a shot of anger like I've had an injection. "I heard she died in a fire, Mrs. Washington. Can you tell us about that?"

She looks over my head as though images will appear on the wall behind me.

"True. That's the way my Chantel went. There used to be an outhouse in the yard. We didn't use it 'cause we have plumbing. I tole those kids over and over to stay outta that place 'cause it was nasty. Smelled nasty, ya know what I mean?"

"Yes."

"I don't know why, but they like playing in there. Beats me. Anyways, that's where it happen."

"In the outhouse?"

She nods wearily. "Chantel go in there and somehow, don't know how, maybe she playing with matches, the thing go on fire."

"Why didn't she come out?"

"That's a mystery. Only thing I can figure is it locked from the outside. Somebody lock her in."

"Would one of the other kids do that?"

"Might. But then they would unlock it they see it on fire. Thing was, was nobody around the day it happen. Chantel home from school with a cold. And that a mystery too. She was with a fever when I left for work that day. I can't figure why she went outside at all, let alone to that stinky outhouse."

I feel a fury building within me and I can tell by the muscle twitch in Cecchi's jaw he feels the same.

"Who called the fire department?"

"Nobody. There weren't no one around that day, neighbors all at work and stuff. When I come home the outhouse was burnt to the ground and then I couldn't find her." Her eyes fill, glisten. "I know it no use calling the police so I call the fire department. I tole them the fire was out so they send a car 'stead of a truck."

"Why was it no use calling the police if Chantel was missing?"

"They pay us no mind. Chantel have to be missing a week 'fore they might talk to me."

"So who came in the car from the fire department?" Cecchi asks.

She shrugs. "Two men. I don't recall the names, if I ever knew. They don't exactly introduce themselves," she says with a snicker. "They go out to the yard and poke all around where the fire was. Then they come back and tell me there's bones in there and I knew. After that a police van come and they took away the bones."

"And how long was it before they identified your daughter?"

"Never. It was as long as never. But I knew it had to be her."

"Wait a minute," I say. "No one ever made an identification of the remains?"

"Nope. I never heard from anybody. I tole the police about it maybe being locked from the outside."

"And?"

"They say they look into it."

"But they never did?"

"I never hear nothing more about it."

"If no one ever identified the remains how do you know it was Chantel?"

"Well, honey, where is she then?"

Right. I feel a bit of a fool for asking the question. "What do you think happened? If there was no one around, and you don't think a kid locked her in, then who did?"

"Gotta be a bad person. Maybe one of the ones Chantel been telling me about."

Cecchi and I glance at each other and my detective's heart is spastic.

"Who? What people was she telling you about?"

"I didn't pay a whole lotta mind to it 'cause Chantel, she always telling stories to pleasure me. 'Course this story wasn't like that. I tole her I didn't want to hear that stuff, to stop, but ever once in a while she try. Now I think maybe she was telling me the truth."

"What was the story, Mrs. Washington?"

She takes a gulp of her coffee, bites her lower lip, shakes her head. Stalling. I can see the guilt in her eyes that she hadn't listened to her child.

"None of it is your fault."

"I shoulda listened."

"It's understandable that you didn't. What was the story?"

"Well, Chantel, she say that some men take her someplace and do bad things to her."

"White men," I say.

"Yeah. That's the other thing. What am I supposed to do about that?"

"It would be hard," Cecchi says.

"It be impossible," she says.

"What did these men do?"

"I don't know exactly 'cause I wouldn't let her tell me. But they was sex things, that much I know."

"Did she say who the men were?"

"She didn't know the names, she say. Except one time when I didn't stop her fast enough she looking in the paper and she show me a picture and she point to this white man and she say he one of the bad ones."

"Did you know who he was?"

"Oh, yeah. That's why I surely didn't believe her, *because* of who he was. Besides everythin' else I work for him a few years back, cleaning house. Well, I work for the Mrs., but still anyone know who he is."

"Who was it?"

"It Mayor Latham."

Twenty-Nine

It's a shock to find out that the mayor, moron that he is, may be implicated in something awful. Something that's looking more and more like some sort of conspiracy and a sex ring.

Latham isn't going anywhere and the day is basically over. It's almost five o'clock. Cecchi and I opt to call it quitting time and drive to the market, as it's our turn to shop and cook. We decided that it wasn't fair for Annette to have to do all the cooking.

I hate this more than life. The shopping part isn't so bad but the cooking sucks. At least I'll have company.

"So what are we going to make?" I ask him.

"I was hoping you had an idea."

"I don't. If I had my computer I could log on to the net and get a recipe."

"Yeah? When's the last time you did that?" he asks.

"Never."

"Funny, that's what I thought."

The carts are outside the market. We take one and go inside.

Cecchi and I have elected to make eggplant parmigiana. Notice there's an *a* on the end of the word. If there's anything I hate more than people (especially waiters) saying *parmigian*, I don't know what it is. Given time I'm sure I can come up with something. I prepare the salad while he works on the eggplant.

"So what do you think?" he asks.

"Well, we now have two kids claiming that bad men did bad things to them."

"And one of them implicating the mayor."

"And Bill Moffat saying 'no one is who you think they are,'" I say.

"And five dead women. You think those murders are connected?"

"I'm not sure about that, but Judy Kempler's murder makes me think they might be. One of them might have been a copycat."

"The one that you suspect that Howard guy of doing?"

It amazes me how Cecchi can remember everyone's name in such a short time.

"Yes. By the way, I saw him today. Sorry I didn't mention it but I couldn't. Jean Ashton was with us. He was coming out of the pet store."

"He see you?"

"I think so. He looked at us then quickly turned away. It could mean nothing."

"But it could mean something. I mean, the guy's a salesman. You'd think he'd want to glad-hand you, keep trying to sell you a car."

Annette comes into the kitchen.

"Hey, there," Cecchi says. "Didn't know you were here."

"And where would I be? I've been lying around like a slug and reading. Delicious."

"See," Cecchi says.

"See what?"

"You can enjoy yourself even if it is a small town."

"Cecchi, you're pushing it," Annette says.

"What are you reading?" I ask.

"A new suspense by Marilyn Wallace. Boy, she's good."

I ask to borrow it when she's finished. I like Wallace too.

"Eggplant parmigiana? Mmmmm."

"Want to help?" I ask.

"No. I get to cook tomorrow night. Hate it."

Cecchi says, "Nobody likes to cook anymore. I love it."

"Oh, please," Annette says. "That's because you do it once a year."

"Twice," he responds.

"Ex-cuuuuse me. Lauren, don't you know about prewashed salad greens?"

"Is that like preowned?"

Annette laughs. "Maybe they don't have them out here."

"There she goes," Cecchi says. "Thinks only N.Y.C. has civilized things."

"I'm with her. But actually," I say, "I've seen those. Sort of expensive, aren't they?"

"But well worth it. You don't have to do a thing. None of that damn washing, and all sorts of greens. I think it's the single most wonderful invention of the nineties!"

"You go too far," Cecchi says.

There's suddenly a racket from the front of the house that sounds like a rocket launch. It's the return of the workers. We go out to greet them.

Jenny says, "You wouldn't believe how much we got done today."

I could say the same but don't.

"It's going to be a great little house," Kip says longingly.

I pretend not to notice her tone.

"I can't wait until we get rid of those minchy windows and put in doors to the deck," Jill says.

"What deck?"

"The one we're going to build," Jenny says.

I see that a lot of new plans have been formed since I was a member of the work contingent.

"Time to let out the animals."

"Oh, God."

"Kip, you know they get along," I say.

"Nora doesn't. Nora hates it."

"So she hides. So what?"

"It doesn't seem fair. Why can't I let her stay in the bedroom?"

"You know why. The litter. Nick has to be able to get to it."

Jenny lets out Theo. She races from one to the other of us, jumping up, tail wagging, trying for kisses. I let her lick my lips.

"Come on," I say to Kip. We go together to our bedroom to let the cats out. They're both asleep on the bed.

"It seems a shame to wake them," Kip says.

I laugh. "Yeah, you're right. They don't get enough sleep. Only twenty hours a day." I take Kip in my arms. We hadn't parted too wonderfully this morning. She seems stiff, unyielding. I back off. "Okay, what's up?"

"I don't know what you mean."

"Kip, please. Are you still sulking from this morning?"

"I don't sulk, Lauren."

She does, actually. Never mind. "Well, you're not very friendly. Can't say that I feel any love coming my way."

"I saw the look on your face before."

No use playing games. "When you said the thing about their house?"

"Yes."

"You really want to move here?" I ask.

"No. But I want to buy a house. For summers." She sits on the edge of the bed.

There's nothing wrong with this. It'd be nice to come here for vacation. But it'll be *her* house, once again. "I can't afford to do that." I sit next to her.

"I can," she says, blithely.

"You don't get it, do you?"

"Know what, Lauren? I *do* get it. But why shouldn't I have the things I want because you can't afford them? Why must we live at your income level?"

She has a point. Still. "Okay, suppose you buy a house. You won't resent having to pay two mortgages, two everything? You won't resent having to furnish it?"

"First of all, it'll be *our* house. And you'll help me pick out everything that goes into it."

"Help you? See, that's not exactly equal."

"You know what I mean."

"Yes, I do. That's the point."

"Oh, forget it then." She starts to get up but I grab her hand, pull her back.

"No. I don't want to forget it. If you want to buy a house then do it."

She moves closer, kisses me quickly. "It'll be fun. We can start looking tomorrow."

"I'm working," I say. "You have no regard for that."

"Yes, I do. I'm sorry. I forgot. Are you any closer to a resolution?"

"Maybe," I say. It's not a lie. We do know more than we did this morning.

"So when the case is over we can start looking."

"Okay."

"It'll be great to have a place we can get away to. Winter weekends in front of the fire."

Panic grips my heart as I see Manhattan drifting farther and farther away. "I thought you said for summers."

"Mostly. But it'll be wonderful to get out of town on winter weekends, won't it?"

"I don't know. I like New York in the winter."

"Not every weekend. But it can be romantic," she says, running a finger over my lips.

I like the sound of that.

She continues. "I see us lying on a plush rug in front of a roaring fire, munching on delicacies . . ."

"Combing each other's hair," I say. This is a joke we have because on the few occasions that lesbians have been portrayed on television they've been shown combing each other's hair. Something I doubt anyone does.

". . . Combing each other's hair," she says. "Taking off each other's clothes, piece by piece and —"

There's a knock at the door.

We jump as though we've been caught in the act that Kip is describing.

Jill says, "Phone for you, Lauren."

"Okay. Don't go away. I'll be right back."

She smiles seductively.

I smile too, hopefully in the same manner.

As I walk to the phone I wonder which of the people I've interviewed is calling me. Has one of them remembered something else? Will someone have the defining piece of the puzzle? The phone is in the living room. I pick up the receiver and say hello.

"It's Stash Volinewski," he says.

I can't help feeling disappointed, as he has nothing to do with the case.

"Yes, Stash. What can I do for you?"

"It's about Jean Ashton," he says. "She's been murdered."

Thirty

We aren't exactly welcome at the crime scene. Several officials have told us to get out of the way. The yellow tape is already up around the house and we've been asked to stand behind it. The only familiar face is the town supervisor, Perini, since this is a different jurisdiction from Seaview.

When Stash Volinewski comes over to us he seems completely bereft. "Why would anyone want to kill her? She was a really great lady, what can I say?"

"Yes, I liked her. I saw her this afternoon." I think of Lee Howard, who saw her too. With us. But why would that mean anything to him unless he found out who I am? "Stash, do you know Lee Howard?"

"Yes. Sure. As a matter of fact he called me about you." I feel a frisson of fear. "Really?"

"Said he wanted to thank me for sending you to him." Of course. I relax.

"I guess you used my name because you didn't know anyone else, right? Were you looking for a car?"

"No."

"I didn't think so but it only dawned on me too late. I'm sorry," Stash says.

"Sorry?"

"In the course of the conversation I gave away where you were living. I'm sorry. What can I say?"

The fear returns. "He asked you where I was living?"

"Let me think."

I do.

"Yes and no. I offered that I'd rented you a house on Spring Lane and then he asked which one, and before I realized that maybe you were investigating him, I told him."

"So he knows which house I'm in?"

"Afraid so."

"You didn't tell him I'm a P.I., did you?"

"Oh no. Never. I did have the feeling he wanted to ask me more about you so I pretended I had another call and got off."

I don't like this one bit. And if Howard did some more snooping he could easily have found out that I was a P.I. Which would mean when he saw me with Jean, he might suspect that she knew something, something perhaps about him.

"How did you find out Jean was murdered?" I ask.

"A mutual friend called me. He heard from Tom, her husband."

Cecchi says, "Do you know how she was murdered?"

"No."

This is important. Is it another Silk Scarf killing or something else?

"Stash, do you see anyone around here you could ask?"

"Sure. I'll ask Perini."

We watch Stash as he approaches the supervisor.

I say to Cecchi, "What do you think about Howard asking about me?"

"Could've been innocent. A real thank-you call."

"Do you believe that?"

"No."

"Me either."

Stash comes back. "Silk Scarf murder," he says. "Jesus. Poor Jean. Why her?"

"Why any of them?" Cecchi says.

"Can I ask you two something?"

"Sure."

"Have you gotten anywhere on the Moffat case?"

"I think we have. I can't go into it because . . ." It's then I realize that my employer is dead. I turn to Cecchi, who I can see has also taken this in. "I guess we're unemployed now."

"No," Stash says. "That's why I asked. I'd like to hire you. I want you to find out who killed Jean."

"You mean you want us to find out who the Silk Scarf killer is?"

"Why not?"

"The police have been working on this for years, Stash. What makes you think we can do any better?"

"What can I say?"

"You know our rates?"

"Jean told me. It's fine."

"Excuse me a minute," I say, and take Cecchi to one side. "What do you think?"

"As the man said, why not?"

"You think we can find this killer?"

"It's all connected, Lauren. I'm sure of that, aren't you?"

"Yeah. I guess I am. Even if Lee Howard didn't have anything to do with killing Jean, somebody knew she was on to something so I guess the Silk Scarf killer could be connected to the child crimes and the Moffat murder."

"That's the way I see it," Cecchi says.

"So we'll take the job then?"

He nods. We go back to Stash.

"Okay," I say. "But you have to understand that we might not get results. This killer has eluded the police for years."

"So you can't do worse, right?"

"I guess you could look at it that way. Maybe we should go somewhere and have coffee."

Stash laughs. "At this hour?"

I look at my watch. It's seven-thirty.

Seeing the puzzled look on my face he explains. "Coffee-type places don't stay open at night around here. Let's go back to my house. You want to follow me?"

He gives us the address in case we lose him, which won't help a bit.

In the car, as I keep my eyes on Volinewski's taillights, Cecchi says, "You think the husband could've killed her, made it look like the Silk Scarf killer?"

"Crossed my mind. Let's not forget, we thought there was something else she wanted to tell us about Ashton."

"Maybe Volinewski can tell us more about the guy," Cecchi says.

"I have a feeling he knows everybody and everything about everybody. Real estate. They know people."

"Think there was anything going on between Volinewski and Jean?"

"It did occur to me but then I dismissed it. I don't know why, but I had a feeling they were only friends."

"We'll have to ask him," he says.

I agree.

We're silent for a mile or so. Then I say, "Do you miss it, Cecchi?"

"The Job? Sure. But I'd rather be doing this than pushing papers in a crummy station house."

I smile into the dark. I'm so happy that I've been able to help him out and get his help in return.

Volinewski takes a right and I follow. It's not long before he takes a left and then another right and pulls up in front of a copse of trees. I park behind him.

We take a path that winds around a small house, probably eighteenth century. He unlocks a door to what appears to be a dining room.

"Let me make a fire," he says and goes over to a potbellied stove. He throws in a couple of logs, and lights the paper and twigs that have been laid earlier. "You'll be surprised how fast this warms up the room. Here, let me take your coats."

When we've dispensed with that and he's put some coffee on, we sit at a round oak table. The room is dense with plants, and the floor is made of cobblestone. The ceilings are low, as they are in these houses. I think it's a nice house but I hope it isn't the kind Kip wants. I'd prefer something newer, but with charm. A long-haired black cat approaches.

"That's Smoky," Stash says.

It's clear to me, as I lean down to pet the cat, that Stash lives here alone. There's a bachelor feeling to the place. I wonder if he's ever been married.

"I can't believe Jean's dead," he says. Behind his glasses, his blue eyes glisten with tears.

"You and Jean," Cecchi says.

Oh, boy. Is Volinewski supposed to understand what that means?

"We were friends," he answers.

So much for what I know.

He smoothes down his unruly mustache. "I've known her for over twenty years, ever since I moved here after my wife died. She had cancer. An old school friend of mine lived here and Marissa and I visited him. We liked it, had planned to move here. Then . . ." He trails off.

"Sorry," Cecchi says.

"It was a long time ago."

"And you never remarried?"

"Sometimes," he says sadly, "there's only one person who's right for you."

Cecchi asks, "Where you from, Stash?"

"New Jersey."

"Me, too," I say.

We exchange the name of our towns and agree that we were glad to leave there. The coffee is ready and Stash gets it. He brings us each a willowware mug and a milk pitcher and sugar bowl in the same pattern.

"What can you tell us about Jean's husband?" Cecchi asks.

"My personal opinion?"

"Right."

"I don't like him. I think he's slippery. Slick. Gives me the creeps."

"Did Jean tell you about her feelings toward Tom?"

"Well . . ."

I can see that Volinewski is having trouble with breaking

her trust. "I know it feels like a betrayal to tell us anything Jean might have told you in confidence, but it's different now."

"Yes. I can see that. This is to help her, I know. Well, she didn't love him anymore. She said he'd changed in the last five years or so. She thought it had happened around the time he got on the town board, which was also the time their last child left home, so she didn't know which it was or maybe both."

I ask, "Did she say how he'd changed?"

"He'd become remote, distant. Almost secretive, she said. They hardly ever talked and she was lonely. That's why she'd begun spending more time with her cousin Billy."

"Did she suspect he was into anything . . . illegal or underhanded?"

"It's funny you ask that," Volinewski says. "She did."

We wait for him to continue.

"It had to do with his computer." An expression crosses his face that resembles disgust.

"What about it?"

"Hell, I do feel like a rat telling you this. I know, I know. I have to. She wasn't supposed to ever touch it, the computer, but once when he was away, she did. He had it password-protected but it only took her about four tries before she figured out it was their son's name and birthdate."

I say, "People should use random numbers, that's the hardest thing to crack. What did she find?"

"Pictures. Pornography. She was shocked and disgusted."

I can understand her feelings but this is hardly unusual. Many men and some women like pornography.

"The thing was," he says, looking down at his coffee, "they were of children."

This is different.

"Were they explicit?" Cecchi asks.

He raises his head. "She didn't know because she didn't actually look at them. She was so shocked she turned off the computer. Said it was instinctual. She got more of an impression than anything else. He must have downloaded them from the Internet."

"Probably. She never looked again?"

"No. She talked about having me look at them but we didn't get around to it."

Now I understand why Jean couldn't tell us. She probably didn't want to implicate Tom no matter what she felt about him. He was, after all, the father of her children. And talking about child pornography to strangers was too much for her.

"What do you make of Ashton having those pictures?" I ask.

"I think he's one sick bastard."

"Do you think he could've murdered her?"

"Do I think he was capable of it or do I think he did it?"

"Both."

"Yes to the first, no to the second. He apparently has an alibi."

"Which is?"

"He was with Perini and some of the other board members, having drinks at the Sound Vista. Before that he was at Town Hall."

"So you think it was the Silk Scarf murderer?"

"I do."

"But why? Let's review the women he's killed." I take a notebook from my purse, flip it open. "The first one was Marilyn Hillard, in her thirties. The second Connie Kuerstiner, about twenty. The third Ceil Cantwell, in her sixties; then Judy Kempler; and now Jean. Did you know any of these women, Stash?"

"All of them," he says sadly.

"What, if anything, do they have in common?"

"It's hard to say off the top of my head, what can I tell you? I'll have to think about it."

I turn to Cecchi. "We need to look more closely into the Hillard and Cantwell murders." To Volinewski I say, "It's been suggested that the second murder, Kuerstiner, might be a copycat."

"Why?" he asks, naturally.

"Your friend Lee Howard was mentioned."

"You've been talking to Edith, haven't you?"

I nod.

"She has a bug up her nose about Lee, always has."

"Then you don't think he's capable of murder?"

"Look, what can I say? I suppose anyone is capable of murder. Me, you, you."

"I've never subscribed to that theory," I say.

"Especially when it's a serial," Cecchi adds.

Volinewski says, "But a copycat would be different, I suppose."

We agree.

"Lee isn't my favorite person but I can't imagine him . . . I guess you never can imagine anyone you know."

"That's true. If there is a serial killer here, he's probably someone you know. I gather you know many people."

"In my line of work you do get to meet buyers, sellers, a mixture; yeah, a lot of people."

"And there isn't anyone you can think of who you can see as a killer?"

"It's hard. Let me think about it. You have to separate the people you don't like from people who you think might do something like that. I never thought about it before."

"See if you can make us a list of possibilities."

"That'll be hard. But I'll do it. I want to help as much as possible."

"So, what do these women have in common? We have to find this out. They were all different ages. Did they look alike in any way, Stash?"

"I guess they all had dark hair, now that I think about it. Of course Ceil Cantwell was going gray. Judy Kempler and Marilyn had kids but the others didn't. I don't know off the top of my head. I have to think about it."

"Jean had kids," I say.

"I meant little ones."

"You think about it and we'll talk again. I'm sure you don't want anyone knowing you've hired us, and that's our policy anyway."

He gets our coats and we shake hands, say good-bye.

As Cecchi and I drive home he says, "Kiddie porn. It fits, doesn't it?"

"You mean with the deaths of the kids?"

"Could."

"I'd like to get my hands on that computer," I say.

"Yeah, I bet you would."

It's only then that I realize I never went back to the bedroom to tell Kip I was leaving. Oh, boy. I'm in for it.

Thirty-One

Stash cleared away the dishes from the table. Was he crazy, getting involved like this? But his motive was right, after all. Still, now he'd have to be seeing these people all the time. He'd chosen real estate because you didn't have to be intimate. You talked to people but it was all superficial. This, he was afraid, wouldn't be.

Smoky rubbed against his legs. "What is it, Smoke? You want some food?"

He went over to the cat's bowl. "You crazy? Your dish is full. Eat that or forget it."

Now he had to make lists, for Christ's sake. You couldn't tell who might be a murderer or who might not be. That was for damn sure. And it was true what he'd said, how could you not suspect those you didn't like? He was bound to put Perini on a list, for instance. And Luke Latham. He hated his guts. But he knew he wasn't a murderer. It wouldn't be fair. He had to think about it carefully so he didn't implicate someone because he didn't like them.

He turned on the faucets and began to wash the mugs. He thought about Jean and how much he'd miss her. It was horrible that she was murdered. She had understood him. And she was one of the few people he let into his life in any way. Even though he knew the others it didn't affect him the same way. He knew them only superficially. And that was another thing.

He turned off the water, dried his hands on the plaid dish

towel next to the sink, put it back, and walked through the hall into his room with the television. A few months ago he'd had a satellite dish installed, one of the small ones, and now he got tons of channels and more than eight hundred movies a month to choose from. He picked up the hefty program magazine and flipped through to today's date, ran his finger down the grid that showed what was playing at this hour.

He finally found something that was going on in a few minutes, *Stealing Beauty*. It was either that or *Broken Arrow* but he hated those shoot-'em-up things, so no contest.

The room was small, filled with comfortable but overstuffed furniture, and the big fifty-two-inch set he'd indulged in overpowered the room. But he didn't care what it did to the space, he wanted comfort and he wanted a big screen and it was his house, his decision. He smiled to himself, thinking that this was one of the great pleasures of living alone.

People were always asking him if he was lonely, wasn't he sorry he hadn't married again. Assholes. If he'd wanted to marry he would've. But he preferred his solitude, preferred not having to consult another person about every decision. He couldn't picture a wife putting up with this room, for instance. Even Marissa would've hated it.

He sat down on the orange velvet couch, took the box of Godivas from the table, lay back with the box on his stomach, and got ready for the movie. The tail end of some awful thing with the inevitable car chase was playing now.

It wasn't a question of *if* they'd find out, it was a question of *when*. So why hadn't he told them? Stupid. He'd tell them tomorrow. Or should he phone them now? It's not like he could pretend that he'd forgotten. What was he going to say, what reason would he give them? The truth was best, he guessed. He'd say he was afraid.

Stash sat up to go for the phone but the movie ended and although there'd be some filler before *Stealing Beauty* went on, who knew how long he'd be kept on the phone? But if he waited until the movie was over it'd be too late to call.

Well, what the hell were they going to make of it tonight, anyway? He lay back down and opened the box of candy, picked one that looked like a cream, and settled back into the pillows. Tomorrow was soon enough. Sure. He'd tell them tomorrow.

Thirty-Two

Surprisingly, Kip doesn't appear at all angry with me when we return. In fact, she's loving and concerned.

"Was it horrible, darling? I know it's worse when you know the person, even if it's on a limited basis."

"I didn't get to see her. But, yes, it's awful that it happened."

"Of course it is. I feel terrible even though I only met her that once. You haven't eaten, have you? Sit down. We kept some eggplant warm for both of you."

Cecchi and I exchange bewildered glances and take our places at the table. Kip actually serves us. I'm extremely suspicious of her behavior but I can't figure out what's going on.

She sits down opposite me and says to Cecchi, "It's awful that Lauren got you out here for no reason, not that we're not happy you're here, but now there's nothing for you to do."

Oh, boy. I get it. She thinks we're unemployed and she's thrilled.

She goes on. "I'm going to call that nice real estate agent tomorrow, honey, and ask him to show us some houses, okay?"

"Kip . . . I . . ."

To Cecchi she says, "Lauren's afraid the house will be all mine and she'll have nothing to do with it."

Cecchi smiles and nods because he knows what's coming.

"Kip."

"What?"

"The nice real estate agent?"

"Yes?"

"He's hired us."

She slumps back into the chair. "Hired you."

"Right. We're still employed."

"I don't believe this," she says.

So we're back to the same old problem. Money. "You should be glad for us," I say.

"Don't tell me what I should be."

"Kip, I promise, as soon as this case is solved I'll go house-hunting with you."

"That's a meaningless promise. By the time we have to go back to the city you could still be on this case."

Of course this is true and I have no defense.

"Excuse me," she says, and gets up from the table, goes into our bedroom.

The others are staring at us from the living room.

"What?" I say.

They turn away.

Cecchi says, "What're you going to do?"

"Meaning?"

"You going to stay on the case?"

"You kidding? Of course."

"I think she's pissed," he says.

"I *know* she is. I have to make a living. She can't have it both ways."

"Which are?"

"Me contributing financially and also doing stuff with her when she wants me to. I can look at houses another time."

He shrugs.

I've lost my appetite. "This is primo, Cecchi, but . . ."

"I understand."

"I think I'd better go in to her."

"Yeah." In a whisper he says, "Sometimes I think marriage sucks."

"Me, too." I get up and leave.

Nick and Theo are under the coffee table, doing their

nose-to-nose thing. Nora isn't visible. At the door to our bedroom I debate what the protocol is here. Do I knock? It is *our* room, after all. Still, the manner in which she entered it seems to dictate that I'd better. I feel like I'm in a *Masterpiece Theatre* series.

There's no response even after I try several times so I go in. She's lying facedown on the bed.

"Kip?" I say, sitting on the edge. We're right back where we were before Volinewski's phone call. Well, not exactly . . . there's no hint of anything sexual now.

"What?" she says, muffled.

"We have to talk about this."

Abruptly she turns over. "I'm sick of talking, Lauren."

"I am too but I don't know what else to do."

"I'm going to call other real estate people and I'm going to look at houses. And if I find something I like and you don't have time to see it, well, then it's too bad."

"That's a terrific plan," I say. "So mature."

"Stop it," she says.

"Well, what should I do then? Give up work so that we can look at houses *you're* going to pay for?"

"What should *I* do? Not look at houses because you can't contribute?"

"I don't see why you can't look at houses and then when you see something you like I'll look."

"Get real, Lauren. When you're on a case you don't have time for anything else. You can't look at houses at night, you know?"

"I'll find time."

"You don't know yourself at all, do you?"

"I think I don't know you."

"What's that supposed to mean and don't ask me what word I don't understand."

I stand up. "You've turned into an unfair person."

"I don't know what that means either."

"You seem to want everything your way. I'm willing to look at houses but —"

She barks out a laugh. "*Willing*. That's great."

"You know what I mean. Listen, Kip. I have to make a living. I'm sorry you don't like what I do and I'm sorry it takes up the kind of time it does but I'm not changing careers."

"I know, you're unemployable at anything else," she says, snidely.

"Well, I am. And as I always remind you, being a P.I. was your idea."

"Yes, dear, you do *always* remind me. Oh, Lauren, why did you have to get involved in this goddamn case?"

"Let's not go over that again. I have to make money. This is pointless. We're going round and round and not getting anywhere."

"Oh, we're getting somewhere," she says, mysteriously.

But I don't bite. Instead, I behave in an absolutely adult fashion and slam out of the bedroom.

Of course the others have heard the door and are all staring at me when I come back into the living room. I want to go out, which is what I'd do in New York City, but where is there to go here? I grab my coat and gloves.

Cecchi says, "Where you going?"

"For a walk."

"Want some company?" Jenny asks.

"No, thanks."

Annette says, "It's awfully dark out there. Is it safe?"

"It's not Tenth Avenue at three in the morning," I say.

"That's safe," counters Annette.

The others laugh. I manage a smile, zip up my jacket, and tell them I'll be back soon, then open the door to the freezing cold. I'm already regretting this but I have to save face. Our outside lights are on so I can see my way down the steps and part of the driveway. Then halfway to the end of the drive it becomes quite dark. When I reach the street it's pitch. This might be one of the dumbest ideas I've ever had. Why don't they have streetlights here? It's uncivilized.

There's a sharp wind that stings my face, whisks around my body, drills through my jeans. I hear the sound of waves breaking on the shore. Normally I love the sound but tonight its constant rhythm spooks me.

Carefully, one small step at a time, I go toward the end of the street, where I know there's a parking lot to my left and to my right is another street, which goes to Sound Avenue. It takes me an inordinately long time to get to the end of the street, which I only realize I've done because I can hear the water differently and feel more space around me.

There's no moon or stars to help light my way. I stop. Should I take the right or go back home? I feel I can't return yet. Why am I being such a baby? And why do I feel frightened? As I'm about to take the right turn, car lights snap on and I'm directly in them.

It's impossible to see the car and when it revs its motor it takes me a second to understand that it's headed for me. At the last possible moment I dive to my right and roll until I'm stopped with a thud by an unidentified obstacle. I stay flat on the ground and listen.

The car screeches to a halt. Silence. Then it starts up and slowly, lights off, makes its way down the street. I can see nothing but I guess when it reaches the corner it accelerates, and with a squeal it turns and speeds off until I can no longer hear it.

But I can't hear anything because the roar of my breathing blocks out all other sound, even the waves and wind. I'm completely disoriented and afraid to stand up even though I'm sure the car is gone. And then it hits me as though I hadn't realized it until this moment. That car was trying to kill me. The person in the car was trying to do this. Who was it? And why?

I grow colder as I lie there and know I have to move. I reach out a hand until I touch whatever it was that stopped my roll. I guess it's the trunk of a tree and I grab hold with both gloved hands and pull myself up to my knees. The ground is sandy and moves beneath me. Slowly I rise, hit my head on what probably is a branch. I stand there for about two hundred years and then take my first step away from the tree and toward where I think the street is. I move along by tiny increments, sliding my feet through the sand. My detective's heart does a dirge.

Eventually, after bumping into bushes, brambles, and beach grass, I feel the change from sand to cement under my shoes. The darkness drapes my shoulders, weighing me down. I try to be reasonable, intelligent, logical. If I'm facing the water, which I must be, then to get home I should turn left.

It takes a long time, as I constantly look over my shoulder for car lights and stop every few inches to listen. Finally, I see the lights on our house and I almost scream with joy. I hurry, careful not to fall.

I run up our drive and the stairs, fling open the door, practically fall into the living room, and close the door behind me.

When I turn around the others jump to their feet with various shouts.

"Oh, my God."

"Who did that to you?"

"What happened?"

"Oh, nothing," I say.

Thirty-Three

At ten in the morning, Cecchi and I are on our way to interview Alison. After having a check run by a friend on the Job, the only person who has a jacket is Von Elder. But it's a juvenile and it's sealed. Still, we have to question her.

The night before, after realizing I had scratches and bumps, I convinced everyone that I'd wandered off the road and fallen in some brambles. I hadn't wanted to give any more ammunition to Kip (or worry her).

Annette and the others had fussed over me, cleaned up my cuts, and then when Kip and I went to bed we'd been civil to each other, but things were still tense then and this morning.

Until now I hadn't been alone with Cecchi. "So what really happened?" he says.

"Somebody in a car tried to run me over."

"What?" He's alarmed. "You sure?"

"I couldn't be surer. Whoever it was took aim and rushed me. I jumped to the side and rolled."

"But how could anyone even know you'd be coming out?"

"Just lucky, I guess."

"Where did it come from, the car?"

"It was in the parking lot at the beach."

"If they were on surveillance for you why would they be parked so far away? You can't see the house from there."

"Don't know. None of it makes much sense. What's the point of killing me?"

"Jesus, Lauren. I don't like this."

"Me, I love it."

"Be serious. Maybe you should get off this case."

"Now you be serious."

"What the hell have we stumbled into here? More and more I think it's something big."

"I couldn't agree more. Bill Moffat's murder, and I'm convinced that's what it was, was the tip of the iceberg."

We discuss the variables of the case until we pull up in front of Von Elder's house. She's at the door when we go up the steps.

"I've been expecting you," she says.

After I introduce her to Cecchi and we sit down, she explains.

"I was twelve," she says. "My best friend was Caroline. It doesn't matter what her last name was . . . is. I guess we were in love with each other. I'm not a lesbian but at that age, well, you know how girls get sometimes."

I nod.

"Anyway, she had a harridan for a mother who wanted to keep us apart. She must've suspected our feelings for each other and it frightened or threatened her in some way. My mother couldn't have cared less. Well, Caroline's mother gave her an ultimatum to stop spending any time with me and that's when we planned it." She swallows hard, looks down at her shoes.

"Planned what?" I urge.

"To kill her mother."

Neither Cecchi nor I show any sign of shock, as we don't want to put her off.

He says, "And did you?"

"Yes. You can't imagine how hard it is for me now to understand or believe I did such a thing. Anyway, obviously we were caught and we each spent time in a juvenile institution. When we were released part of the condition was that we'd never see each other again. And we haven't.

I have no desire to anyway. So now I guess you think I'm a killer."

"No we don't," I say. And I don't. It's a surprise but I'm convinced she had nothing to do with what's going on now.

Cecchi says, "You should probably tell the local police because if we found out, they will too."

She laughs lamely. "That doesn't automatically follow around here. I think I'll take my chances. I don't believe the local police would be as understanding as you two."

"Did Bill Moffat know about this?" I ask.

"Yes. He's the only person I've ever told and he was wonderful about it."

We thank her for telling us, reassure her that we won't report it to anyone else, and leave. As I start the Jeep I ask him what he thinks.

"Funny, I've heard much worse stuff my years on the Job, but it shocked me."

"Me too," I say. "What if we'd heard somebody in the city tell us that?"

"Might've been different. Don't know. I wonder how they did it."

"I didn't want to ask her," I say.

"No, me neither."

We're silent for the rest of the ride.

We pull up in front of the town hall, ready to interview Julian Perini. As we walk up the path Cecchi says, "I'd be real surprised if this dude tells us anything helpful."

"You never know."

Perini's secretary is a woman in her forties, hair dyed blond and worn like June Allyson. She has bright, brown polish–colored eyes, and her makeup is too heavy.

"We have an appointment with the supervisor," I tell her before she can ask, and give her our names.

She smiles sweetly. "Take a seat. I'll tell him you're here."

We do and she does.

"He'll be with you in a moment."

And it isn't more than a minute before the intercom on

her desk buzzes and we hear a tinny voice telling her to send us in.

Perini rises from behind his desk and comes around it to shake our hands with his enormous ones.

"Nice to see you again," he says.

We both agree.

Today he wears a gray pin-striped suit, and the dome of his head is shiny, like a frozen ski slope.

We take our respective seats; he goes back behind the desk. "So, you're both Italians, huh?"

Cecchi says he is.

I say, "I'm half German."

"So am I," Perini says eagerly, as though this makes us pals.

I smile.

"First generation?" he asks.

"Second," Cecchi says.

"Third," I answer.

"Me, too. Third," Perini says.

I have to switch things so I'm doing the questioning. "Have you always lived here?"

"No. I grew up down Island. Babylon. Moved here forty years ago though. I guess they accept me. Well, they made me supervisor." He laughs, the same way he did at Bill Moffat's funeral, too long and loud for what he's said.

I eke out a smile. "Mr. Perini, we're here —"

"Call me Julian," he interrupts.

"Okay. We're here because we've been hired to look into the murders of Bill Moffat and Jean Ashton."

"Now hold on. Moffat was a suicide. And Ashton, well, that was the work of the serial."

"Our employer doesn't believe Moffat was a suicide."

"Who's your employer?"

Cecchi says, "We can't tell you that."

Perini nods as if he'd known that all along. "Moffat was a suicide. That's what the M.E. ruled it."

I take out a notebook and make a note to interview the M.E.

"What are you writing?" Perini asks, alarmed.

"A note to interview the M.E. Who is he, or she?"

"He. What do you want to interview him for?"

Cecchi and I glance at each other because it's such a stupid question.

I say gently, "Well, it's a natural thing to do. We should have done it sooner."

Perini grunts. "Ed Conroy's the M.E. Conroy's Funeral Home in Seaview. And Ashton? You're going to try and solve the Silk Scarf murders?"

"We're going to try and solve Jean Ashton's murder and since she was strangled the same way . . ." I shrug.

"Unless it's a copycat," Cecchi adds.

Perini says, "People been trying to solve the Silk Scarf murders for years. You think you got a chance?"

"You never know," I say. "And then there are the children," I throw at him.

"The children?"

"Are you aware, Julian, that four children have had accidents and died over the last few years?"

He stares at us. "So?"

"Two of those children claimed that they were molested by some men."

He crushes his heavy eyebrows together over the bridge of his nose. "I never heard anything about that."

"And one of them was a child of one of the Silk Scarf murder victims."

"So what are you saying?"

Cecchi says, "We believe these things are all tied together."

Perini thinks. It's not a pretty sight. "So then you don't consider as true that the children had accidents?"

"Right."

I notice little beads of sweat on the dome of Perini's head and he runs a hand over it, wiping them away. "So let me get this straight now. You think the Silk Scarf murderer killed these children?"

"Could be, but not necessarily," I say.

"So what do you think then?"

I decide it's time to say it out loud to someone. "We think there might be a group of pedophiles around here."

"Pedophiles?"

I can't decide whether he doesn't know the word or he's simply dumbfounded by the idea, so I wait, not wanting to insult him.

"Pedophiles," he repeats. "You think there's some men around here who like to do dirty things with kids?"

"Possibly."

"And you base this on the words of kids? Hey, now. We aren't gonna have one of those witch hunts here. Oh, no." He stands up.

"Some *dead* kids," I remind him.

"Alive, dead, I don't want any McMartin stuff going on in my jurisdiction. I think you'd better leave."

"Julian," I say. "Don't you want this thing solved? And if there is a pedophile ring, don't you want it stopped?"

"There's no ring out here."

"How can you be so sure?"

"I know this place, these people."

Cecchi says, "You've got a serial killer, why not pedophiles?"

"No, no. That's different."

I almost laugh. "You mean you can accept that you've got a murderer in your midst but not child molesters?"

"That's right," he says seriously. "Hey, what makes you think the serial didn't kill these kids?"

"It's a possibility," I say, trying to be agreeable but not believing it for a moment.

"The M.O. is different," Cecchi says. "And usually a killer of grown women doesn't go after kids."

"Wait a minute," Perini says. "Then you're indicating we got a situation here which is producing more than one killer?"

It does sound bizarre in an area this small. But we must never forget Cabot Cove. Or St. Mary Mead, for that matter.

I say, "There is a possibility of more than one killer."

Perini begins to breathe heavily and I watch his jowly

face turn first pink then almost crimson as he yells at us.

"This is disgusting, what you're saying. I got enough troubles with the serial and now you want me to believe that there's a secret group here, preying on kids? You're off your rockers. What do you know, you two wiseguys from New York City? That sort of stuff goes on down there but not here. You're maligning some of the most upstanding men in our community. I want you two out of here, now."

We stand up at the same time, thank him, and leave.

In the car, Cecchi turns to me. "You got it?"

"Of course I got it."

"So he knows about it."

"Absolutely. Now all we have to do is find out *which* upstanding men he was referring to."

"How do we do that?"

"The local newspaper," I say and start the Jeep.

Thirty-Four

Julian Perini wasn't sure who he was angrier at, those two from New York or the others. It had never occurred to him that there were any murders involved. Well, maybe there weren't, although it did seem like too much of a coincidence if two of the kids said something about it and then they died.

This wasn't what he'd bargained for, not at all. The whole thing was bad enough but he liked the money. He sat down at the desk and thought of his father. A little late to be thinking about him.

Albert Perini had told his sons, "Don't never do nothing for money that you wouldn't do for no money."

Julian thought now he should've taken that advice. But this wasn't the first time he hadn't heeded his old man. His father worked like a slave his whole life and what'd he end up with? Zilch. He didn't want to be like him.

The business brought in a good amount and his salary as supervisor helped, but Ramona liked to live high, and to be honest, so did he. And then there was Beverly to buy nice things for. So when this deal came along, hell, why not? What did it mean to him, after all? But nobody said anything about killing kids.

He put a fat hand on the phone and thought. Did any of the others know about this? What if they all knew but didn't want him to know? Why would that be? If they knew and were keeping it from him, it was because they knew he'd go bonkers. So if he let them know that now he knew, somebody might get scared and . . . and what? It was hard to even think about this. Nah, he couldn't see anybody trying to kill him.

He lifted the phone from the cradle, started to punch in a number, then returned the receiver and sat back in his chair. But if somebody was popping kids, then that somebody wouldn't have any trouble taking him out, would they?

If he let one of the others know he was wise to what was going on, then that person might tell one of the men involved, and he didn't even know who they were. All he knew was they were important and that had been all he wanted to know.

But now, now was different. Maybe he should find out who they were. Ask casually, like he was curious. Maybe that would look suspicious and he'd be a candidate for murder. Still, it would be good to know who he should look out for.

He reached for the phone but didn't pick it up. If he didn't say anything to anybody nobody would know he knew anything and he'd be safe.

But what about those two P.I.s? Nah. And what was some girl gonna find out, anyway? Nothing to worry about from them.

The best thing to do was what he'd always done in situations like this: Nothing. Yeah, nothing was the best way to go. He buzzed his secretary.

"Yes, sir?"

"The doughnut cart come around yet?"

"It's down the hall."

"Get me two jellies, okay?"

"Yes, sir."

Do nothing, he thought, and nothing happens. That's what his father should've told them. Hell, he'd been doing that as supervisor for the last ten years. Why do anything about anything now? Screw that.

Thirty-Five

The name of the local newspaper is *The North Fork Times* and it comes out once a week, on Thursdays. We've discovered this by looking at one in a 7-Eleven. The offices of the paper are farther down the Fork, in Millquogue. The masthead tells us that the managing editor is a man named Colin Maguire. There is, of course, the chance that he's involved in this mess and won't be helpful at all but it's a gamble we need to take.

The paper's offices are in a Victorian house set back off the main road. It's recently had a coat of yellow paint with white trim. We go up the steps and cross the broad porch to an ornate door. I feel as though I should knock but I know better.

A young woman sits at a desk in what was once a foyer. From what I can see, which is the top half of her, she's dressed in a blue sweater with a lighter blue turtleneck beneath it. Her brown hair is straight and touches her shoulders, like mine. She has a pinched face, as though it's been inside a gargantuan clothespin.

"May I help you?"

I tell her we'd like to see Maguire and then she utters the worst five words in the English language: "Do you have an appointment?"

"No, we don't," Cecchi says.

"Well, I'm afraid you can't see him unless you have an appointment."

He takes out his new P.I. license and flips it open in front of her.

"What's that supposed to be?" she asks.

Cecchi looks at me, bewildered. He's not used to this. Showing his NYPD badge had been an easy entrée for him.

He says, "It's not *supposed* to be anything. What it is is my P.I. license."

"Your what?"

"We're private investigators," I fill in.

She doesn't look impressed. "And you're investigating Mr. Maguire?"

"We didn't say that," Cecchi responds.

I can see by the muscle jumping in his cheek that he's getting annoyed.

"So, what are you investigating then?"

"We can't tell you that. Would you ask Mr. Maguire if he'll see us?"

"If I don't know what you're investigating then —"

"Look, this is official," Cecchi cuts in.

Oh, boy. I touch his arm.

The woman says, "You know something, mister, it's not official. You think you're Suffolk County police or what? You're two gumshoes. I know how it works."

I hate television. I glance at her nameplate. "Look, Ms. Parr, you're right, in a way. But we are on a case and we do need to speak to Mr. Maguire. At least ask him if he'll see us, okay?"

She stares at me for six hours. "Well, all right, I'll ask." She wheels her chair backward and when she gets up I see that she's wearing black leggings and brown lace-up Tretorns. I know the brand because I have a pair like them.

Cecchi says, "Is this how it is?"

"Yeah. Worse sometimes. You have to face it: We don't have the same clout you had on the NYPD."

"And they think we're scum, don't they?" he asks forlornly.

There's no point in lying. "Sometimes. Some of them do."

He looks crestfallen. I pray this isn't going to change his mind about working with me. Ms. Parr returns.

"Well, I don't know why but he'll see you." Translated this means we're scum and I can tell that Cecchi knows it.

"He's through that door," she says.

"Thank you," Cecchi says, sarcastically. Then to me, "They don't even escort you in."

"It's not always as casual as this," I say. I don't tell him I once had a secretary hanging on to my legs as I stormed some guy's office. I knock on the door. A male voice tells us to come in.

Colin Maguire sits behind a large oak table that serves as a desk. He has dark hair with gray at the temples and a graying mustache. His eyes are a cerulean blue and he has nice, even features. He wears a white shirt, sleeves rolled up.

He rises, shakes our hands, and asks us to sit down. I notice some photos on another table next to him. One is of two small girls and another of a woman in what looks like a minister's robe and collar. I point to it.

"Your wife?"

He turns to look at the picture as though he has to check to make sure it is. "Yes, Annie. She's a Universalist minister."

Good. With a minister for a wife I find it hard to believe that this man would be involved in anything as vile as what I suspect is going on here. It's not an absolute, but it bodes well.

"And those are my two girls, Sara and Lizzie. We call her Z because Sara couldn't say her name when she was a baby."

I try not to smile. It's so funny the way people tell you these things about their children, as if it is important that you know the facts.

"Patty said you're private investigators. I know you can't tell me who hired you but what case are you on?"

"Both the Bill Moffat murder and Jean Ashton's."

He frowns. "I thought Moffat was a suicide."

"We don't think so," Cecchi says.

Maguire makes a note. "Interesting. And Ashton? Isn't she a victim of the Silk Scarf murderer?"

"Maybe."

"You going after him?"

I don't like it that Maguire is interviewing us. I don't answer. "Mr. Maguire, we'd like to know who you think are the most upstanding men in this community."

He raises both black eyebrows. "You think one of them is the S.S. killer?"

I smile enigmatically. "I didn't say that."

"I suppose you won't tell me why you want to know?"

"Can't right now."

"But you have a theory or something?"

"Or something," I say.

"If you have anything that involves the bigwigs around here, I'd like to know it."

"What if when we're sure we give you an exclusive."

He laughs. "We only have one rival. Rag city. But how about, you have an item you call me right away."

"Deal."

"So you want the names of only men?"

I look at Cecchi, who nods. "Yes."

"Here's the thing. We have a feature we do which is People of the Year but they're not necessarily who you might be looking for. Give me a better profile."

"That's not easy because I'm not sure. How about this. Suppose the town supervisor referred to some men as upstanding, who'd they be?"

"Julian? Well, they certainly wouldn't be most of the People of the Year types. I mean, one or two might fall into that category, but they wouldn't be confined to that."

"So you pretty much know who he might mean?"

"Hell, yes. That's easy."

Maguire has told us to come back in an hour and he'd have a printout of the names we've asked for.

"I think we should call our employer and update him, don't you?" I reach for the car phone.

"Good idea. But what's the update?"

"Oh, that." What *is* the update? "What do we know today that we didn't know yesterday?"

"One thing only. That probably some important figures in this community are involved in something that's disgusting."

"So what does that have to do with Jean Ashton and the S.S. killer? Nothing, right?"

"Not sure. I think Moffat found out something and maybe told her."

"No. She would've said so. Is the S.S. killer involved with the kiddie-porn people?"

"Possibly," he says. "I hate to lay this on you, Lauren, but it's likely that Ashton was killed because she hired us. I only think that because somebody tried to kill you."

I feel a jolt when he says this. My second language is denial and I'd already pushed that episode way below the surface of my mind. "Wait a minute, that doesn't make sense. If the killer of Ashton did it to get me off the case then why would he need to kill me? Nobody knew Volinewski hired us but Volinewski, and he has no reason to kill me."

"Maybe he told somebody. Call him."

I look in my notebook and punch in his office number. Someone else answers and then transfers the call to him.

"Spring Realty," he says.

I identify myself and ask him if he's told anyone that he hired us.

"Well, no. But a lot of people saw us go off together."

This is true. We'll have to try to remember who was at the scene. Before I get a chance to update him he says, "I was about to call you."

"What's up?"

"I forgot to tell you something when you asked me what the murdered women had in common."

"Oh?"

"Yeah. I mean, it's coincidence but the fact is, I either sold or rented them all their houses."

"You forgot that?"

"I know it seems crazy, but what can I say? Thought of it after you left. I don't know what it could mean, what it would have to do with anything, but I thought I should mention it."

"You did the right thing. Okay, Stash. Thanks a lot."

"You find out anything?" he asks.

"Since last night? Nope, not yet. But we'll be interviewing some people today."

When I hang up I tell Cecchi about Volinewski's connection to the murdered women's houses. He raises one eyebrow.

"This he forgot?"

"Could happen. More important is to try to remember who was at the murder scene last night, who saw us leave with him."

"Right."

I snap my fingers. "You know, I wondered why he was there."

"Who?"

"Lee Howard. I think it's time to pay him another visit."

Thirty-Six

Howard gets up from his desk, hand extended. "I thought you'd be back," he says, smile in his voice. Today he wears tan slacks and a blue sweater that matches his eyes.

I take his hand, introduce Cecchi, and we sit down at his desk.

"Can't get that Jeep out of your mind, right?"

"Not exactly," I say and take out my P.I. license. "Mr. Cecchi and I are private investigators."

He looks surprised but I don't believe him. "You investigating car dealers?"

"No. Mr. Howard. Why were you at the Ashton crime scene last night?"

"I told you I live in Millquogue and I'm a volunteer first aid worker."

My detective's heart sinks. It's a perfectly sound reason. Still, he did see us leave with Volinewski.

"You told me last time you were a police buff but you didn't mention that you were a volunteer worker."

"No? Well, I am. So you're investigating Jean Ashton's murder then?"

Neither of us answers him. We want to get him rattled.

He stares at us, fusses with some papers on his desk, looks at us. "You working on the Silk Scarf murders? That why you were asking me all those questions last time about Connie?"

"You stay at the crime scene long?" This will be easy to check.

"Actually, no. I left right after you did."

So he'd been aware of us.

Cecchi says, "Why didn't you say hello if you knew we were there?"

"Well, Mr. Cecchi, I didn't know *you* and it wasn't exactly a social occasion, now was it?" There is no affect in his eyes. They are like beach glass.

"Where'd you go when you left?" I ask.

"Well, I'll tell you but I want you to know that I know I don't have to answer any of your questions."

"That's right, you don't."

"So this is the last question I'm answering. I went home."

"You have something to hide, Lee?"

He laughs. "I know the trick of calling me by my first name, too."

"So *do* you have something to hide?"

"No."

"Then why won't you help us with our inquiries?"

"Maybe if you tell me what you're investigating I will. I know you can't tell me who you're working for."

"We're investigating Ashton's murder."

"So then," he says, "you're investigating the Silk Scarf killings?"

"That's not what I said."

"That's who killed Jean," Howard says.

"Maybe."

"So, you're investigating Ashton's murder and you're only *maybe* after the Silk Scarf killer and you're questioning me. Why?"

"You saw us with her."

"I did?"

"In front of the Pequash Diner. I believe you were coming out of the pet shop."

"Oh, right. Yeah, I did. But, hell, it didn't even register until now."

There's no way I believe this.

"You looked right at us," I say.

He shrugs, boyishly, helplessly. "So what exactly is it that you want? You think I killed Jean?"

"Did you?" Cecchi asks.

"Yes," he says. "Just kidding."

"You think it's a joke?"

"No, but you guys must. I mean, what's the point of asking me a question like that? If I did am I going to tell you? No. You here because of Connie? Edith's been talking to you, hasn't she? Bitch," he says under his breath. Then he catches himself, pastes the smile on his face. "I didn't kill Connie and I didn't kill Jean. In fact, folks, I didn't kill anybody. Now I have work to do."

"Why'd you lie to me about Kristin Baxter?" I ask him.

He doesn't look up. "I think you'd better leave."

"She says you harassed her. It's easy to check, you know."

"So check it out then."

We have no legal right to go on questioning him, so we leave.

In the car I say, "He lives alone so there's no way we can validate where he went after leaving the Ashton scene."

"He's a creepy guy. Who's Kristin Baxter?"

I tell him.

"Who's Edith?"

I explain.

"And she thinks Howard killed her niece?"

"Convinced. I have a hunch, Cecchi."

"About what?"

"About Connie. And since we need to talk to the M.E. anyway I think we should do that now."

"Okay by me. Tell me your hunch."

I do.

The M.E. and the funeral director at Conroy's in Hallockville are one and the same. I hate these places. So who likes them?

We get in to see Edwin Conroy right away. He's not at all like the movies would portray him. Nothing odd or spooky-looking about the guy. He's in his fifties and lanky, with a receding hairline, ordinary brown eyes, and a large nose. He wears a dark blue suit, white shirt, and blue tie.

We sit in his office in comfortable chairs facing his huge walnut desk. His large hands rest on top, the long fingers laced together.

"Have you been the M.E. for a long time, Mr. Conroy?"

"Fifteen years. Took over from my dad."

"So then you've been in on the Silk Scarf murders from the onset?"

"That's right."

"Would you say they were all done by the same killer?"

He tips his head back, revealing a scar on the end of his prominent chin. "Yes, I'd say they were all done by the same perp."

"What about Connie Kuerstiner? Do you remember her?"

He looks offended. "Of course I remember her. I remember all my people."

Uh-oh. Now he sounds spooky. *His people.*

"She was the second vic," he continues. "Anyway, I'd be unlikely to forget Connie."

"Why's that?"

"She was pregnant."

I look at Cecchi. My hunch was right. I wonder why Edith hadn't told me this.

"And that was reported to everyone?"

"It depends who you mean by everyone, Miss Laurano."

"The police, the family, the . . ."

"No. Not the family. An aunt was her only family and we didn't think it necessary to tell her, as Miss Kuerstiner was unmarried."

I'm astonished.

"You look surprised. This is a small town. We do things a little different here. There was no reason for the aunt to know. What purpose would it serve?"

"Didn't this make Lee Howard a prime suspect?"

"Why? They were engaged to be married. He knew about

her pregnancy, of course. But he was going to do the right thing, so what was there to be suspicious about?"

"And there was nothing different about her murder from any of the others?"

"All exactly the same M.O."

"So you don't think Kuerstiner, or any of the others, might have been a copycat murder?"

"Didn't look like it to me."

"Were any of the other vics pregnant?"

"Nope. I'd remember that."

"Let's move on to the children," I say.

"The children?"

I enumerate the children who'd died from so-called accidental deaths. His jurisdiction covered only three of the four.

He sighs. "Terrible tragedies. But all accidents."

"Was there anything unusual about any of them?"

"Do you mean their deaths or their bodies?"

I take a flyer. "Their bodies."

"Well, Bebe Kempler's body was real disturbing."

"Meaning?"

His big ears begin to turn red. "She showed signs of having been interfered with. You know."

"No. What exactly do you mean?"

"She was only nine, after all," he says.

"Mr. Conroy, please say what you mean."

"Her vagina was not intact. Her hymen had been broken and her vulva was swollen. She'd been sexually abused."

"Did you tell her family or did you think they should be spared?" I say, angrily.

"It went in my report. I assume the police told the family."

I don't.

"What about Bill Moffat? Suicide?"

"Oh, no. He was murdered."

Thirty-Seven

"Murdered?"

"That's correct."

"But the police declared it a suicide."

He looks at me. "Murder was what I put in my report. Manual strangulation. I can't help what the police declare." He nervously adjusts the small knot of his blue tie.

"Mr. Conroy, didn't you say anything to anyone?"

"Like who?"

Cecchi says, "Like the police? Didn't you question them as to why they ignored your ruling and declared a different one?"

"My job ends when I hand in my report." He pushes some papers around in a meaningless way.

"But you're the M.E. here. Why didn't you tell someone else?"

"No one asked me until you did."

Both Cecchi and I are flabbergasted.

"So what you're saying then is that somebody strangled Bill Moffat and then hung him?"

"That's the way it looked to me."

"And what about the Silk Scarf murders?"

"What about them?"

"Were they done the same way? Was it manual strangulation first and then the scarves tied around their necks?"

"No. They were straightforward. What you saw was what you got."

"In your opinion," I ask, although I don't have a whole lot of faith in it, "could the Moffat murder and the S.S. murders have been done by the same person?"

"Why not? Different M.O. but who says they'd be the same. The S.S.'s were all women. Moffat was a man. Stronger. Could've fought back."

"You mean there was no sign of struggle from the women?" Cecchi asks.

"There was from a few. I'm saying that Moffat could fight back harder, being a man."

"How about Jean Ashton? Any sign of struggle there?"

"I haven't finished yet, but so far, no."

"Are you sure there was nothing at all different about Kuerstiner?" Cecchi asks.

"It's a while back but I can look in my files." He stands up and goes to a four-drawer file cabinet, pulls out the third drawer, riffles through the contents. "Here we go."

Back at his desk he opens the manila file and runs a finger down the edge of the page as he reads. "There *was* something different. How could I've forgotten that? The knot was in the back. The knot of the scarf."

Cecchi and I look at each other. So maybe Lee Howard did kill Kuerstiner.

"I'm sorry I forgot that." He looks sweaty, nervous.

"You can't be expected to remember every detail," I say.

"Well, I should of remembered that one."

I agree but don't say so. "You said there were signs of a struggle by some of the vics. What were they? Skin under the nails?"

"No," he says. "Nothing useful, like anything we could get DNA from. Bruises and such."

"And the children? Was there any sign of struggle on any of them?"

"They were accidents."

"They appeared to be accidents. Was there?"

"No."

"But there was the abuse on Bebe Kempler. You said you reported that."

He nods.

I look at Cecchi to see if there's anything else he wants to ask. He almost imperceptibly shakes his head no.

We get up and I thank Mr. Conroy.

He says, "I'm not going to get in any trouble, am I?"

"Frankly, I don't know. It seems unusual for an M.E. to allow the police to rule suicide when he's ruled murder."

"So who you going to tell?" Beads of sweat dot his brow like seeds.

"Tell? I'm not going to tell anyone. But I am going to ask."

"Who?"

"The police, of course."

"Look," he says, voice trembling. "I wish you wouldn't. I shouldn't have told you about that. I'll get in trouble. You don't know how it works around here. This is a small place and we operate different from New York City."

"I'll say."

"Seriously. There are factions. We have a situation here."

"Why don't you tell us about the situation?" Cecchi asks.

"I can't. When I said that Moffat was a murder, I don't know, it popped out."

"Maybe because the better side of you took hold."

"Jesus," he says and puts his head in his hands.

Cecchi and I sit down. We wait. After a while, Conroy looks up at us. His face has fallen like he has a worn-out lift. "I have two boys in college," he says, as though this should explain everything.

We wait.

"Do you know what it costs now to send even one to college?"

"Are you saying that you took money from someone, Mr. Conroy?"

He presses his lips together and nods. "It was wrong, I know. But Christ, it paid for a whole semester for Mike. That's my younger son."

"Who paid you?"

"Don't know. It came in an unmarked envelope with a typed note, no signature."

"What did the note say?"

" 'Bill Moffat was a suicide.' "

"That was it?"

"That was it. That and six thousand dollars in cash. It's the only time that it ever happened. What would *you* do?"

"You're asking the wrong people," Cecchi says.

"Did it come through the mail?"

"No. No postmark. Put in my letter box outside."

"And still you wrote in your report that it was murder?"

"No. I lied to you about that. I got scared and . . . I don't know. I tried to cover but then you said —"

"Yeah, we know what we said. So nowhere does it say officially that Moffat was murdered?"

"Nowhere."

"What about the abuse of Bebe Kempler?"

"Oh, Christ," he says. "I don't know why I told you that."

"You mean it wasn't true?" I'm surprised.

Conroy's eyes fill with tears. "No, it was true."

"So what's the problem?"

"I didn't put it in the report. The money for Moffat wasn't the only time. I needed it for Rick, my other son."

Cecchi asks, "Same deal, the way the money came to you?"

He nods.

"What did the note say?"

" 'Ignore your findings.' It was five thousand, that time. What's going to happen to me?"

I find Conroy disgusting. We rise. "Officially? I don't know. I guess that'll depend on how this investigation turns out and if Moffat is exhumed. Or something comes out about Bebe. Personally? I wouldn't want to be you trying to sleep."

Cecchi and I pick a restaurant in the middle of Hallockville called Joe's. The weird thing about the spot is that it has pictures of movie stars all over the place. And standing cutouts of people like John Wayne and James Dean.

I say, "Are we supposed to believe by the photographs that these people have eaten here?"

"Beats me. If we are, I don't."

"Me either. So why are they all over the walls?"

Cecchi says, "You want to make it a mystery, solve the movie star scam or what?"

Our waitress approaches and for a moment I consider asking her but change my mind because I figure she won't know, and I also don't wish to engage. We each order a burger, a Diet Coke, and she leaves.

"So who paid Conroy?" Cecchi asks.

"The killer, I'd guess."

"Or those who hired the killer."

"The kiddie-porn people?"

"Wait. You think we got two different killers here? The S.S. and the one who killed the kids?"

"Why do they have to be connected?" I ask.

"Conroy. The money, the notes."

"They had to do with a kid and Moffat. Nothing to do with the S.S. killer."

"You're right. So the Moffat and the kid killer are the same. The S.S. killer is different. That what you're saying?"

The waitress brings us our drinks.

I take a swig of Diet Coke. "I don't know what I'm saying."

"You're suggesting two killers, Lauren."

"Maybe not."

"Since when does a serial of grown women kill kids? You said that yourself."

"Maybe when someone knows who he is and needs something else taken care of."

Cecchi looks at me for six or seven years. "Let me get this right. You're saying that somebody, maybe in the porn group, knows who the S.S. killer is and gets him to do the kids and Moffat?"

"I guess I am."

"Jesus," he says. "Who?"

"I don't know."

The burgers arrive and they look wonderful. I can't believe how big they are or how inexpensive. I guess it would be cheaper to live here.

"Who was the first murdered woman?"

I take out my notebook, flip the pages. "Marilyn Hillard. She was in her thirties. Happened about four years ago." I close my book.

"That's it? That's all you know?"

I feel a bit ashamed that I haven't followed this up. I nod.

"This isn't like you, Lauren."

"So much has been happening," I offer lamely.

"I think we'd better find out more about Marilyn Hillard."

What we discovered when we went to the library and looked at back issues of the papers was that Hillard lived alone in Seaview and was a waitress at a local restaurant, now defunct. Her obit mentioned parents but they lived in Florida.

Now we pull into the parking lot of Spring Realty. Volinewski said he'd sold or rented to all the vics. Cecchi is beginning to like him for the perp. I say no.

When we enter, Volinewski is sitting at his desk. He looks up and seems flustered to see us here, which is odd, considering he's hired us. Maybe Cecchi's right.

"Nice to see you both," he says, rising and extending his hand. "Here, sit down."

There's one chair and he drags another over from someone else's desk.

"So any news?" he asks in his cheery way.

"Tell us what you know about Marilyn Hillard," I say.

He repeats her name, looks blank for a moment, and then remembers. "Oh, her. Yes. Terrible, terrible." He shakes his head.

"Did you rent or sell her the place she lived in?"

"It was an apartment. I rented it to her. Listen, I hope this isn't going to get out. I mean, that I'm connected like this. It could hurt my business."

"How's that?" Cecchi says.

"Well, if people know I've rented or sold to all these murdered women . . . what can I say, isn't it obvious?"

"You mean they'll think you killed them?"

His face goes white, like a peeled almond. "No. That's not what I meant."

"What *did* you mean?" I ask.

"I was thinking nobody'd want to work with me, that's all. But now that you mention the other idea, that's possible too."

"Tell us about Marilyn Hillard," Cecchi says.

Volinewski has lost it. He runs his fingers over and over his mustache, twitches, blinks, wiggles around in his chair. "What can I tell you? Look, *you* don't think I killed these women, do you?"

"No," I say.

Cecchi doesn't answer but Volinewski doesn't seem to notice.

"I rented her an apartment, that's all. Well, no, that's not all. Oh, God."

"What is it?"

"Marilyn was a waitress but she also cleaned houses. She cleaned mine. That's how come I found her the rental. I don't do a whole lot of rentals but I happened to know about this one."

"How long after you rented her the apartment was she murdered?"

"Not long. About a month."

"And the others? How long after you rented or sold to them?"

"That varied. Like my dear friend Jean. I sold Jean and Tom that house over five years ago."

Cecchi says, "So you knew two of the women apart from real estate transactions. Any of the others?"

"Let me think. No. No, I didn't."

"How about Bill Moffat, you sell him his house?"

I didn't think he could get any whiter but he does.

"I don't believe this," he says, more to himself than to us. "I did."

I wonder about the children now but before I get a chance to ask Cecchi says, "How'd Hillard come to clean house for you?"

"She was recommended. It's hard to get good help here."

"Who recommended her?" I ask.

"Ah, let's see. You know I don't recall. No, wait a minute. I do. It was Tina Rendel."

My detective's heart does a samba. "Any relation to Jim Rendel, the head of FEAG?"

"Yeah," he says. "His wife."

Thirty-Eight

"It was the FEAG thing that threw me off," I say to Cecchi as we drive back to the newspaper to get the list from Colin Maguire. "I couldn't see anyone killing anyone because of fast food."

"I understand. So what do you think now?"

"I think Jim Rendel is involved up to his eyeballs."

"I like him for the S.S. murders," Cecchi says.

"Me too. And what about the kids who supposedly died of accidents? And Moffat? Also Rendel?"

"I don't know. We don't know that these two series of murders are connected."

"I thought we did."

I park in front of *The North Fork Times* offices.

"I'll run in," says Cecchi.

Something nags at me. I know this feeling, as I've had it before. There's something obvious that I'm not connecting. It's usually an idle phrase that someone said, or an observation that didn't compute right away.

Cecchi is back with a printout. The list is fairly long. We hunch together and look it over. They are who you'd expect, doctors, lawyers, judges, businessmen. Most of the names are unknown to us. But a few stand out.

> Luke Latham, the mayor of Seaview
> Julian Perini, the supervisor

Phil Dawson, owner of the paper
Vreeland, owner of the car dealership
Tom Ashton
Stash Volinewski
Jim Rendel

All the upstanding men. What do they have in common besides being on this list? And what did the chief of police mean when he indicated we were maligning them? I'm positive he wasn't referring to them all. He had a group in mind, but who? Lee Howard is not on the list. I wouldn't expect him to be. One tumbler falls in place.

"Cecchi, I think I know what's been going on."

"From this list?"

"Well, in a way. Who would you say is the weakest link on the list?"

"Not sure. I didn't get to meet all the ones you did."

"I haven't interviewed him, but I have a feeling that Tom Ashton would be the easiest to break down. He's all bluster. And let's not forget about what Jean told Volinewski. The pictures on his computer."

We look at each other, silently agree. This isn't what's been nagging at me but it'll have to do for now.

I've briefed Cecchi on the way over to Ashton's house so he knows exactly what I'm after, what to ask. We sit in the living room and I feel sad, as the last time I was here, Jean was alive. Ashton is furious even though he let us in. I'm not sure he knows he didn't have to.

"Mr. Ashton, we're sorry about your wife but we need to ask you some questions," I say.

"Make it quick," he says.

"We need the names of everyone in the group."

"Group?"

"We know about the child pornography group."

"I have no idea what you're talking about. I think you'd better leave." He looks like a cornered animal.

"We know who some of them are, but not all."

"Did Jean put this idea in your head? I know she was the person who hired you to look into Billy's death."

"Don't you want your wife's murderer to be caught?"

"Well, of course I do. But what's that have to do with some pornography group?"

"Everything, I believe."

"You mean you think someone in the group killed Jean?"

It isn't exactly an admission that there's a group but it's close enough for me, and for Tom Ashton's face to turn red.

"Possibly," I say quickly. "You have a computer, Mr. Ashton?"

"Doesn't everyone?" he says, snobbishly.

"What kind do you have?"

"A Micron. Why?"

"I'd like to see it," I say.

A frown creases his brow. "What the hell for?"

"Would you show it to us? Turn it on? Let us wander through the files?" I smile sweetly.

"No. What the hell do you know about computers, anyway?"

"Because I'm a woman?"

He doesn't answer. But I know this is what he meant.

Cecchi says, "We know that some of the children involved were Freddy Moffat, Chantel Washington, Bebe Kempler, and Mary Lavin."

I say, "I'm surprised you used Freddy Moffat. Didn't she recognize you? But perhaps that's why you had to have her killed."

He jumps up. "Now wait a damn minute. I didn't have her or any of the others killed."

Another quasi-admission. But I leap on it. "In that case, don't you think you better tell us about it?"

"Oh, Christ," he says and sinks back into his chair. "I can't believe Jean did this to me."

I can't believe this narcissistic reaction. Well, maybe I can.

"If you cooperate with us now, Mr. Ashton, it'll be easier

for you down the road." This is totally bogus as we have no authority. But from my experience I know he isn't thinking straight right now.

"You have to believe me that I thought they were accidents."

My detective's heart says, *Yes!*

"We believe you," says Cecchi.

"I mean, nobody ever said anything about killing those kids. I don't even know who did it."

"Want to tell us who was in the group?"

"What's going to happen to me?"

The question of the day!

"Tell us who else was in this group," I say.

He begins to name names, some of which I recognize from the list Maguire gave us, including Rendel's. This is a surprise, since a killer of grown women isn't usually interested in kids.

"Jim Rendel was part of the group?"

"Well, he never seemed too interested, but he'd watch stuff. Didn't even take any pictures."

It occurs to me now that Rendel probably wanted to be "one of the boys," make himself seem *normal*. Jesus.

"The Seaview chief of police knew about this, didn't he?"

He nods.

"And what, you all paid him to keep quiet?"

"Yes. And it wasn't cheap either."

I'd like to slap him.

"The thing is, the thing you have to understand is I never did anything to those kids. I watched and I took some video, some stills, that's all. But I can tell you the ones who did."

"Good," I say. Somehow he thinks he's not as sick as the others because he didn't actively participate. We let him think this so he'll tell us more.

"Got any ideas who killed the kids?"

"I don't think it was any of us. We thought it was weird they died but we also believed they were accidents. Nothing happened to the other kids."

"The other kids?"

"Jesus Christ, you think the ones who died were the only kids involved?"

"Make a list," I say.

When we leave I call the state police from the car phone. They'll pick up Ashton, Chief Wagner, and the others immediately.

"What about Rendel?"

"Let's go see him."

News travels fast in small towns, and when we arrive Rendel has heard and has barricaded himself in his office with his secretary, Betty Fitzpatrick, as a hostage. It's clear now that he's the Silk Scarf killer so nobody doubts that he would find it easy to kill Betty.

There's only one person who doesn't believe he's the killer: Tina, his wife. It's unusual for a serial killer to have a wife but when he does, the wife never believes it's possible.

The state police have arrived and there are sharpshooters on the roofs of many buildings. It's only a matter of time. The main thing now is to keep Betty alive.

Cecchi and I are on the sidelines as the negotiations are conducted through a phone setup. The head of the troopers puts down the phone and calls out to the crowd:

"Anybody know a Lauren Laurano?"

Oh, boy. I can't believe what I'm hearing. I step forward and identify myself.

"He wants to talk to you," the trooper says.

"Me?"

He shrugs.

"Okay." I take the phone. "Rendel?"

"You bitch," he says.

Very nice.

"Something you wanted?"

"Yes. I want you to come in here and I'll let Betty out."

My detective's heart and my personal heart drop to the pavement. "Why?"

"Because this is all your goddamn fault."

"I didn't kill those women, Mr. Rendel."

"You coming up?"

"No."

"Then I'm going to kill Betty."

I hear a scream in the background.

"Wait," I say. I cover the mouthpiece and fill in the trooper.

He says, "We can't let you do that."

I have to admit, I'm relieved.

"Stall him. We have a shooter getting into place who thinks he can get a shot through a window."

Mind don't fail me now. "Rendel?"

"You coming in?"

"Why'd you start killing when you did?"

"Come in and I'll tell you."

Funny, I'm not at all tempted. "No. You tell me first. Then I'll come in. Was it because of your mother?" Isn't it always?

"Don't you say a damn thing about her."

Yeah, it was his mother.

"Why'd you kill Connie Kuerstiner?"

He laughs. "I'll never tell."

I expected him to deny it. But maybe . . .

"Look, Laurano, you have five minutes to get in here or I'm going to kill Betty."

I tell the trooper. He motions to stall.

"And what are you going to do with me when I come in?"

"I'm going to make you understand it all."

Oh, yeah. "Rendel, I do understand."

"Don't bother, Laurano, I know what —"

There's a sharp crack and then a sound like the phone has fallen. Betty screams. The trooper tells me the shooter got him. I hand back the phone.

It might not seem like much but I feel weak in the knees and have to sit down. Cecchi comes over, puts an arm around me. "You okay?"

I tell him I am.

"So which one of those mutts in the porn group killed the kids?" Cecchi asks.

"I don't think any of them did." The nagging piece has fallen into place. "I think it was another of Chief Wagner's deals."

"Meaning?"

"Remember the M.E. said Kuerstiner had the knot in back?"

"How could I forget? You saying the chief killed Kuerstiner and the kids?"

"No. He was protecting the killer and using him at the same time."

"Rendel?"

"No, not for those."

"Who then?"

I tell him.

We find him having lunch at the Paradise in Seaview. He's alone in a booth and when we join him he tries to pretend he's glad to see us. But I can see in those gelid eyes that he knows it's all over.

By this time the others have been arrested, including Chief Wagner, so he has to know it will all come out.

"Good soup?" I ask as I sit down across from him and Cecchi blocks him in. We both have our guns drawn and in our laps.

"Yeah, great chowder. Want a taste?"

"No, thanks."

"I guess you know why we're here," Cecchi says.

He smiles. "Why don't you tell me."

"Have you heard about the arrests?" I ask.

"Yep."

"Then you must realize Wagner squawked like a chicken."

"Well, he will, but it's too early for you to know what he has to say, the peckerhead."

"So, why Moffat?"

"Moffat was getting too close."

"And me? Was it you who tried to run me down?"

"Yep. So, how'd you figure it out?"

"A little luck and recalling your great love of children."

Howard laughs. "Yeah, that was a piece of cake for me.

Wagner saved my ass after Connie, and then I guess I saved his. Never did know what it was all about. I took my orders from Wagner and carried them out." He finishes his soup and puts down his spoon. "Now what?"

"Now we turn you over to the state police since the police here are of no use."

Cecchi says, "There's one waiting right outside for you, Lee. In case you were thinking of dumping us."

"Crossed my mind," he says.

"Sorry," I say, get up, walk to the door, and invite the state trooper in to join us.

Thirty-Nine

We have had a celebration that the case is closed and that the Js' house is now in a state where they can begin thinking about what they really want to do. They can also put in some furniture. Jenny will be making beds from door shutters, for the frames and . . . oh, I don't know . . . I don't quite understand, but I know it's clever.

As we undress for bed Kip says, "I saw a great house today."

"Tell me about it."

She laughs. "Why? You don't care."

There is no getting away with anything when someone knows you so well. "I care." I think I do. I like it here, I have to admit. "It would be only for weekends and summers, right?"

"Right."

"If we were closer, if things felt better between us, I don't think your buying a house would bother me." I get into bed.

"Really?"

"Yes. I hate that I'll never own anything, that everything is in your name, but I can understand that you'd like to have a house here."

"And do you understand that I'd think of it as *our* house, the way I think of Perry Street as our house?"

"At least I pay something in the city. Kip, this inequity doesn't work."

"Do *we* work, Lauren?"

"Meaning?"

"Is it over between us?"

My lover's heart thuds. "Is that what you want?"

"Don't answer a question with a question, please." She gets in next to me.

"Okay. It's not what I want and I didn't think you did either. We told the therapist we didn't want it to end."

"No, it's not what I want," she says.

"So neither of us wants it to be over. And we agreed that my having an affair was not grounds for divorce."

"Then what difference does it make who owns what, who has the money? God, if we were heterosexual, this wouldn't even come up."

"But we're not. We're two women trying to make a life together and our incomes are disparate."

"Right. That's all it is."

"Then why are you so distant? Cold?"

"Sex," she says.

"Sex? What sex? We don't have any."

"Exactly."

My heart does a swan dive. I've been wondering when this would come up. It's not that I don't want to make love with Kip, it's that I'm afraid. Will it be as it once was? Will I remember what she likes? Will I think of Alex?

Kip sits up, stares at me. "Tell me the truth, Lauren. Are we victims of L.B.D.?"

The dread lesbian bed death. "I hope not."

"Sex has always been the underpinning of our marriage. We've never been close without it."

"So what should we do?" I ask.

"I'm not sure. But I know that we can't be totally intimate with each other unless we're physically intimate."

I know this is true. "Maybe we should make a date . . . an appointment."

"I think we should do it."

"When? Now?"

"You don't have to look so horrified."

"I'm not, I'm . . . I don't know . . . it seems so sudden."

"Sudden? You call nine months sudden? You're not over her yet, are you?"

"Please, Kip, it has nothing to do with her. I'm afraid, that's all."

"You think I'm not? Wondering every minute if you'll compare us, wondering if you'll think my body's old and disgusting."

I see how pained and frightened she is. I touch her face. "I'd never think that."

"Why not? I don't have the elasticity of someone her age."

"Neither do I. Kip, I didn't like the fact that she was so young. It bothered me."

"Oh, that bothered you. Not that you were cheating on me, but the fact that she was a child."

"I didn't say that. Both things bothered me. Kip, I love you, when are you going to believe me?"

She mumbles, "I wish I knew."

I can't believe how much I've hurt her. How could I have been so selfish? "Please, Kip."

"What?"

"Look at me."

She does. "I'm sorry I'm so awful about this, Lauren."

I gather her in my arms, hold her close, whisper in her ear. "Please believe that I love you, because I do. I've never loved anyone as much."

"What about her, the infant. Did you love her?"

We've been through all this before but I know it's incumbent upon me to make her feel secure. I *did* love Alex in a way; nothing that was deep or solid; nothing rivaling my feelings for Kip. "No," I say, because there's no way to explain. "I didn't love her."

"That's even worse," she says. "You're an animal." She laughs.

I laugh, too.

"You are," she goes on. "You took this infant and used her for sex. Animal."

"I'm not getting into this," I say.

Her smile fades. "Why? Because it's true?"

"Kip, don't."

"It is true, isn't it?"

"I've told you what's true. I was lonely. I needed attention."

She says nothing. Then, "Right now, we have to make love right now."

I can't believe how scared I am. In a way, it's exciting, almost like I'm with a new person, yet there's the relief of knowing I'm not. I have to do this. I want to do this. I can't move.

We look into each other's eyes.

"What?" she asks.

I don't answer and then she moves her face toward me and our lips touch in a light but thrilling way. We kiss for what seems a long time and I feel the excitement growing within me. In moments we're entangled. Desire overcomes fear and we both sigh when our naked bodies are against one another. I realize now how much I've missed this. As I pepper her with kisses, working my way over her body, I open my eyes and see that beyond the end of the bed, a few feet away, are Nick and Nora.

Staring.

God, I hate it when the cats watch.